Colours of a Cultural Chameleon

Colours of a Cultural Chameleon

Shakti Hannie

A big thanks to Don and Janine for their helping hand along the way

And a big thanks to my family, without whom I would not be who I am today

First edition November 2020

Copyright © 2020, Shakti Hannie

All rights reserved

Cover © Jeroen Rouwkema

Author's photograph © Christelle Perrin

Chapter illustrations © Rosanne Wielemaker

ISBN 9798552300341

www.shaktihannie.com

To my soulmates Jeroen, Robin and Lianne,

to my family, and

to my own little communities around the world

A note to the reader

Dear reader,

This story is about cultural chameleon Kamala who lives and travels in different countries around the world. To allow you to delve in completely, I have provided descriptions of the flavours of the diverse foods and the local clothing. Additionally words spoken in the languages of these countries add colour to her adventures.

I appreciate that not all the readers will understand the *foreign* words used, therefore a glossary section has been added at the back of this book. The glossary has translations, as well as explanations of words that are typical to a country or time-period. For the ease of reading, crucial translations are also provided as footnotes.

I myself am a cultural chameleon and I am always in search of new colours, in every sense of the word. This book however is not an autobiography. It is based on my understanding of what it means to be a third culture kid. Some of the adventures and experiences I have enjoyed on my journey through life form the basis of this book, sprinkled with a dose of fiction. This is what I love about being a writer: the freedom of creating.

I wish you a wonderful journey together with Kamala, through various countries and through the various stages of her life.

Shakti Hannie,
2020

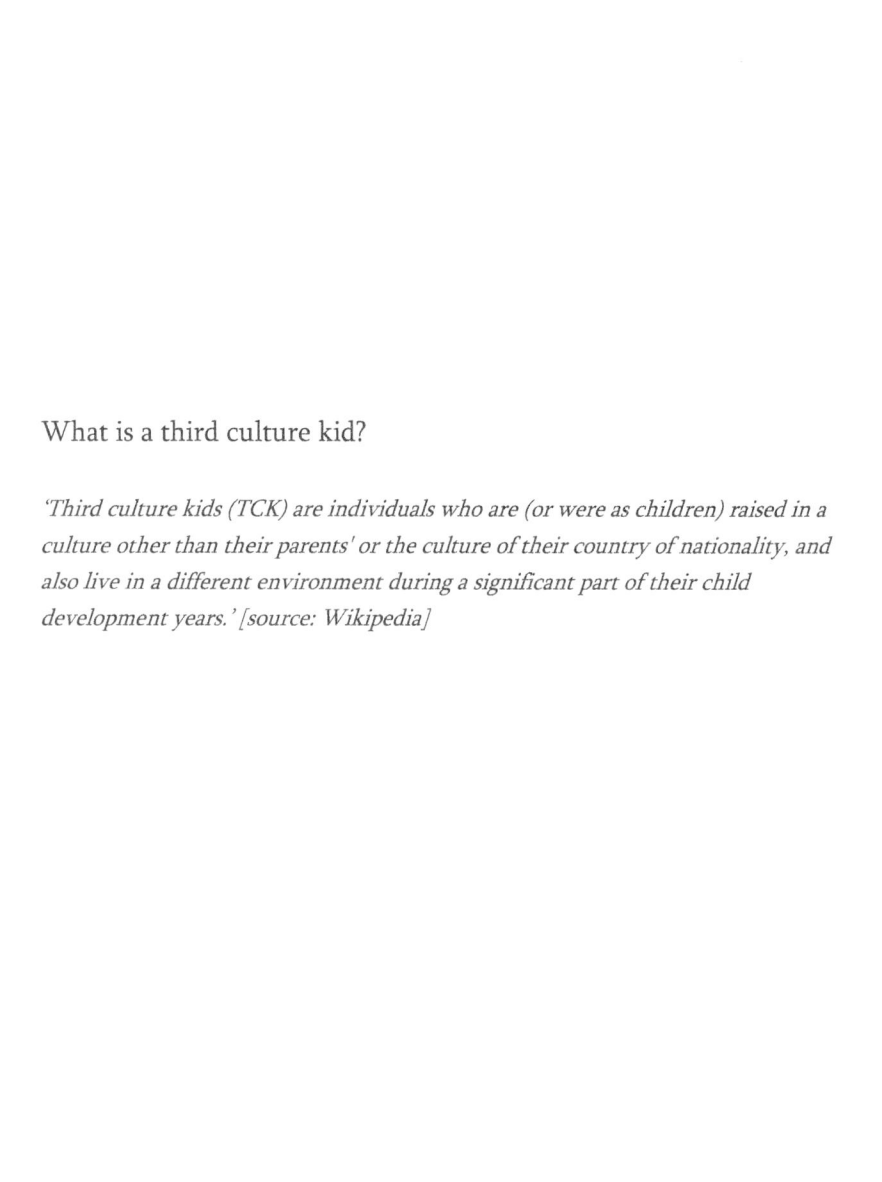

What is a third culture kid?

'Third culture kids (TCK) are individuals who are (or were as children) raised in a culture other than their parents' or the culture of their country of nationality, and also live in a different environment during a significant part of their child development years.' [source: Wikipedia]

Chapters

1. Yeh kya hai? 1
   Everyone clapped 1
2. Kerala Express 13
   Small adventures on long journeys 13
3. Garden at the Graveyard 29
   The labyrinth and the terrace 29
4. The Belgians 41
   Mon Dieu and the Red Devils 41
5. A new chapter is written – tabula rasa 55
   Eighteen and carefree 55
6. Magical Machu Picchu 71
   A Sol for your thoughts 71
7. Travelling unreserved 89
   Faith and fate 89
8. Trust a stranger 101
   Amador & others 101
9. No entry 115
   Joy of travelling 115
10. The Russians are coming 125
    for me 125
11. Communist Cambridge 141
    A cultural chameleon 141
12. Why do I always lose my husband? 155
    Trust 155
13. The next adventure? 163
    A journey into motherhood 163

Glossary

1.
Yeh kya hai? [1]
Everyone clapped

---

[1] What is this? (Hindi)

"Kamala, *yeh kya hai?*" my father asked, seated at our cherry-wood dining table. We lived in a modest working class cottage, with an extensive backyard, in the rural village of Meldert, in Belgium.

"*Kitaab* [2]," I responded, a chirpy seven year old girl. Pa was teaching me Hindi.

My new school-to-be was located in the then 10 million populated capital city of India. It was an English-medium school. English I understood, because Amma, my mother, spoke to me in English. Pa stuck to Flemish, which is spoken in my native Belgium and in neighbouring Netherlands. Most children in my new school in Delhi spoke multiple languages. Hindi was one of them and for schooling purposes I had to learn Hindi.

Pa and Amma met a long time ago, at university in Delhi. There, both learnt to speak Hindi: it was their fourth and fifth language. Amma's mother-tongue was Malayalam, which is spoken in the lush green southern state of Kerala. My fondest place on Earth.

I often heard my parents discuss the topic of our schooling, before the final verdict was conveyed. Sometimes late in the evening, while I was in bed and the door left ajar, and sometimes with raised voices.

"No government school for my children."

"Not all government schools are below standard, Danny. If you had more patience, you too would realize this." Amma wanted us to fully be part of Indian society and to go to a normal Indian school, not to an International expat school. We weren't expats.

"I do not care. They are my children. I do not want your socialist principles ruining their future."

---

[2] Book (Hindi)

That was it. In a few weeks' time, Chettan, my one and a half years older brother, and I were moving across continents: from Europe to Asia. I understood little, but I knew we were not off on a long holiday. This time was different. I recall Lianne, my friend from Kindergarten. She said "Best friends forever", when she gave me a friendship book. I haven't seen her since. On one of those last days at school, I noticed four older children from Chettan's class in a cluster. Their heads grouped close together, and their eyes fixed on me. I imagined they were gossiping about the little sister immigrating to a foreign country. But India was not unknown to me, it was not a foreign land for me, it was a familiar place. I had lived there as a toddler and had often been back to visit my grandparents Ammumma and Muthachan. I was a chameleon, a cultural chameleon. Indeed, I was different from them.

------ When I was a baby, just turned one, I experienced air travel for the first time. Our family — Chettan, Amma, Pa and I — moved to India to live for a while. This was my first visit to my mother's motherland, where we stayed till I turned three. As a three year old I understood and even spoke some Hindi to our caring Didi, our 24-hour help at home. Although she was older than my parents, I called her Didi, meaning older sister. Amma and Pa owned a two-storey house in an upper-middle class neighbourhood in Delhi. I have fond memories of the enclosed garden with grassy patch, bordered by flowerbeds. Near to the house was an area covered by marble slabs where the grown-ups would sit and chat in the pleasant winter sun. We children would play in the front garden and swim in a tiny plastic pool on hot sultry evenings. As a three year old I used to dig up red brick powder and occasionally eat some of it. It tasted good. This is the part of my first period in India that I remember most clearly. All my other memories seem distorted by photographs and 8mm films. ------

This time round, in January '89, we were not travelling to India as a family. Pa was staying back in Belgium. He would join us in a few months' time, since he first needed to finish teaching the academic year at University in Leuven.

On our departure day I had mixed feelings. Would I like living in a big city, where I could not scamper in the woods and countryside? I was apprehensive of what awaited me. On the plane, as I flipped through Lianne's friendship book, I felt melancholy take hold of me at the idea of leaving behind my childhood best friend. On the other hand, the thought of meeting many 'aunties and uncles' and spending loads of time with my cousins Shiva and Vijaya, was thrilling. Sunk in contradicting thoughts and emotions I crossed over from Europe to Asia.

I vividly recall that first month... those chilly Delhi mornings, standing on our first floor balcony, watching life unfold below. Watching people pass by. Men wearing sweaters, dressed up with mufflers covering their head, ears and throat. The smell of burning piles of garbage. A rite every morning. Although January was the depth of Delhi winter, for me with Belgian blood running through my veins, I did not perceive the cold. At midday I would run around wearing a thin sleeveless cardigan and enjoy the mild winter sun.

Those first few months in Delhi we stayed in a three-storey residence shared with Amma's friends, living together as a joint family. In later years, we fondly remembered the times spent with Amma's comrades at G19; G block, house number 19 in Greater Kailash.

On the ground floor lived an elderly couple, aunty and uncle. Uncle had a slight stoop and always wore a woollen shawl. Aunty, I hardly ever saw. I presumed she was stuck in the kitchen. It seemed

Indian wives and maids were perpetually in the kitchen cooking. Whenever I passed their portico, my nostrils filled with the aroma of freshly ground spices or the trace of deep fried delicacies. This made me race up the steps in anticipation of warm munchies. Often I was lucky, Didi too was in the kitchen awaiting my return. Sometimes she asked for a *maalish*, a massage after a long day's work. Didi's hands were big and rough from mopping the floor with a coarse cloth, cleaning the dishes with a metal scrubber and washing the clothes by hand and beating some of them on a stone ledge. Soft fleshy biceps, and sturdy lower arms were the obvious result of turning, squeezing, rubbing fabrics together, rinsing and twisting them dry.

Each floor had its own kitchen and dining room. Our first floor had four bedrooms of which we occupied the one with the private front-facing balcony. Didi prepared food for the first floor residents; all of Amma's age and none had children of their own yet. How welcome we were. A communal house not filled with children's laughter, their screams and jumpy acrobatics, is like a zoo without animals. Here in this communal paradise, I always had someone to talk to and to entertain or be entertained. Standing at the blackboard with a stick and chalk in my hand, I spent hours explaining my world view to anyone and everyone who had the patience or enthusiasm to listen.

After two weeks' of acclimatising to Delhi-life, my school-life started. On the first day I wore a navy coloured box-pleated short, in appearance a skirt. The collar of my immaculately white shirt peeked out from underneath a rust-coloured sweater. On schooldays, this would be my dress code for years to come.

As I stepped out of the rickshaw and onto the freshly swept pavement, I laid eyes on the maiden white Tiny Tots school. My new school to be. The school was located in a fenced-off compound with a playground surrounded by whitewashed one-storey buildings with barred windows. A common sight in Delhi, but peculiar to a Belgian girl. My new classroom was in one of the detached white buildings. Amma led me to room II-A. We paused outside the class's outer wall. As we stood there, I heard voices drift past.

"Amma, I don't want to go," I protested, holding on to Amma's hand. Behind that thick white wall, a new world awaited me. "I don't know anyone, Amma." I hid my face in her *dupatta*.

Amma lowered herself to my height, took my face in her hands and said "All is well Kamala, all is well." She nudged me in.

"Hello Kamala, come along in," the teacher welcomed me.

"Come sit here in the front. We kept a seat for you."

"Kamala, this is Dhamini, your new friend in our class."

"Dhamini, help Kamala okay?"

"Okay, children, open your math book to page…" With this my schooling in India commenced.

I did not have trouble following the teacher's explanations, it was all in English. I did notice children looking at me and whispering to each other. I wondered what they were saying. Maybe, "that's the new girl from Europe" or maybe something else. I wanted to know, or maybe I did not. From each chair hung a colourful chilled water bottle, except from mine. The school bell rang, the teacher left, and the class turned into a circus arena. Dhamini turned around to face her friends at the desk behind ours. They spoke in Hindi. Suddenly, hearing this foreign language spoken all around, I felt awkward. Estranged. I turned and looked out the window, into the empty courtyard. I wondered what Lianne was doing right now.

Next class was Hindi. Aparna madam came in and waved her hand in the air as if fitting a light bulb in a socket. I came to appreciate this school sign, a greeting without words.

"*Namaste Kamala, aaj tumara pehla din hai.* [3]" Aparna madam stood before my desk and smiled at me.

"*Namaste* ma'am," I replied with a faint smile, not able to produce any more sounds or syllables. The intonations were so unlike those I was used to.

Whenever I saw children glancing at me and whispering among themselves, I was reminded of those last days in my school 'De Berk' in Belgium. I did not notice a difference between them and me, but I did feel the odd one out. Here in my class in Tiny Tots, I stood out in more aspects than I realised. Later on in life it was brought to my attention that in Belgium I was a dark toned child and in India a fair skinned girl. At that time, I did not notice the difference and I doubt my classmates did.

In the evening I told Amma how I had felt alienated in school, I did not belong. "Be yourself, no matter what they say," she comforted me.

At school I had to learn to read, write and speak the new language. Amma was at a loss. Hindi was not her mother-tongue. Amma could not help me with my homework, so she decided on home-tuition in Hindi. It was also apparent to her I needed extra attention in Maths. At De Berk I recently learned the 3 times table, here supposedly the children already knew the 10 times table by heart. One of Amma's friends taught Chettan and I Maths through games. I enjoyed these daily visits by Saurab uncle. My Hindi tutor, Ram Sir, was quite the opposite. He was a Hindi purist and a stern man. Utter silence was enforced while I made my

---

[3] Hello Kamala, today is your first day (Hindi)

assignments and he meticulously checked each word I jotted down on paper. My next door neighbour, Tania, assured me Ram Sir was not a strict teacher: "Maybe Europeans see him as strict, but we don't," she said. She then explained further, "he does not use his pencil as drumsticks on your knuckles nor as a wedge in between your fingers. He is quite okay." Ram Sir gave me heaps of homework and I had to learn much by heart. To me, a Belgian girl, the concept of homework was odd.

"Amma, you know, Ram Sir says Hindi and Flemish are family."

"It is called the Indo-European language family tree," Chettan, seated at the dining table corrected me, briefly distracted from his daily dose of The Times of India.

"But Amma, they are so different. Pronunciation in Hindi is tough, Amma. Each letter has two pronunciations. Like k and khhhhh."

"In Hindi those are two different letters, with and without aspiration, Kamala. They are also written differently."

"Yes, just like the Ts and Ds. I hate those, Amma."

"Do you still find it difficult?"

"Yes, the sounds are so unfamiliar and the way I hold my tongue in my mouth is awkward. I get my tongue twisted."

"Tea, three and tree, when Kamala says it, you never know which one she means," Chettan joked.

"Do not be mean," then she looked at me and said, "Yes, I know it is tough, the intricacies of Hindi. Hindi has four different ways of pronouncing the T and four different ways of pronouncing the D."

"Why those two letters, Ma? I wish it had been the K or the M with an added hhhhhh. Or any other letter, but not the T!"

After a few months in Delhi, we moved. Ram Sir and Saurabh uncle's visits relocated to our new home. We stayed in the same neighbourhood. Now, we had the entire top floor to ourselves. It was a pleasantly spacious house, with high windows and high ceilings. The walls were made of uneven plaster with cracks. The first time Amma opened the front door, light filtered through and the breeze played with the dust on the steps that led to the living room. Another few steps up led to the dining room with an attached kitchen. This terraced floor-plan and the 'give through window' in the kitchen, I considered the best part of our new home. At the rear of the apartment were two bedrooms. I shared one with Chettan. Didi helped out and we frequently spent time in G19; it would always remain our joint home. Often I helped Didi gather the washing. Walking on fire, in the mid-afternoon sun, when I ran up to the terrace to check on the clothes. The stone floor burnt the soft soles of my feet. Didi would call for me; she always knew what I was up to. Soon after we moved, Pa started teaching at Delhi University and joined us in our terraced home. Our family was complete again.

Once I had settled at school, I travelled by the white coloured Tiny Tots school bus. Every morning it was the same routine. Waking up at 7am. Bathing with a bucket of cold water and a jug. Sitting down for a hot breakfast, prepared by Didi, and drinking hot milk with a hint of chocolate. I tried to avoid drinking the milk with its disgusting *malai* layer. I preferred cold salted *lassi* instead. Unfortunately I was hardly ever lucky. The other horrible chore in the morning was getting my waist-length wavy hair oiled, unknotted, combed and braided into two braids.

"Ouch Amma, no Amma, please no," I cried, pulling away from Amma's hands, resulting in even louder screams because Amma's fingers got caught up in my knots and some of my hair ended up in her hand. All of this happened while I kept a perpetual eye on the clock. Each day I rushed down the stairs and raced to the bus. At the school-bus stop, other children were calmly waiting with or without their parents. On most mornings me and the bus shared first place and I boarded the bus, on some days I came second.

"What happened today, Kamala? You are very early," an uncle asked me as I stood waiting for the bus one spring morning. I smiled. Amma and Pa had gone to the province of Punjab for a few days; Didi was taking care of us. No morning struggles today. She braided my hair in the evenings. On that particular day, Aparna madam asked me to read aloud the Hindi poem that we had been learning in class. I stood at my desk, picked up the book and started reading.

> "*Ek kauwa pyaasa tha,*
> *Jug me thoda pani tha*
> *Kauwa dala kankar ....*"

After I finished reading the two-page poem about this thirsty crow who dropped stones in a half-filled vessel to increase the water-level so he could have a few sips, I lowered the book and noticed that all my classmates and Aparna madam were clapping.

A giant smile from ear to ear split my face. I felt thrilled. Confident. I lowered myself back in my seat, turned to face Nandini and Aarti and started talking to my new friends-to-be, in Hindi.

Here I was, a seven year old girl with braided hair, confident to conquer this room, this school and confident to conquer this continent.

Confident to conquer the world.

2.
Kerala Express
Small adventures on long journeys

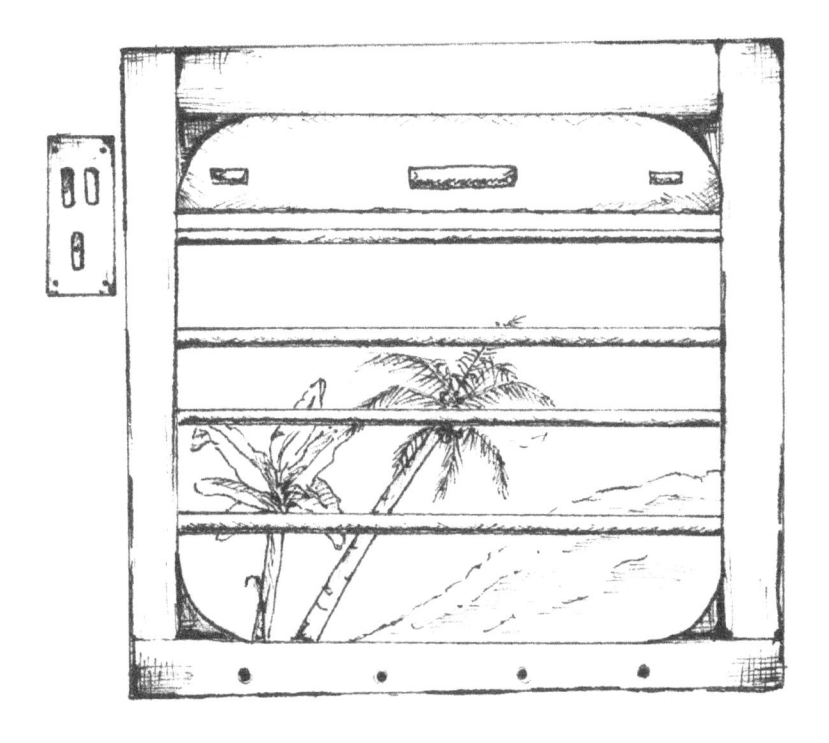

The summer heat was pressing down. I wished we had booked the AC-car, like some of my posh friends did. On the Kerala Express, we would be travelling sleeper class, a 52 hour train journey down south. We were to spend a month in the city of Trivandrum with our grandparents; Ammumma and Muthachan. The Kerala Express passed through the states of Uttar Pradesh, Haryana, Rajasthan, Maharashtra, Madhya Pradesh, Andhra Pradesh and Kerala. I felt an adventure was in its making, though I was dreading the unavoidable delays. I knew, from experience, that as long as the train was in motion a breeze, even if it was a warm one, would give some solace. The waits in vast stretches of no man's land, that is when the stifling heat kicked in. It was unavoidable.

As we made our way through the crowds, I felt the summer vibe fill the platform. Everywhere families were trying to locate their assigned coach, followed or preceded by red turbaned *coolies* carrying their luggage. Chettan, Shiva and I were carrying our own bags. Shiva was Amma's brother's youngest son. Shiva lived in Delhi with his parents. He was one year younger than me. Vijaya, his 3,5 years older sister, wanted to be a doctor. She lived in Trivandrum with our grandparents. Down south she hoped competition would be less and admissions easier.

A *coolie*, carrying a few suitcases on his head and another one in his hand, passed by. Sweat was trickling down his temples from underneath his turban. Behind him walked a well-fed chubby boy in shorts, followed by what I presumed to be his sister. The rest of the well-to-do family followed suit. The *coolie* located their coach and stopped to unload. A fellow *coolie*, exiting the coach, helped him slide the luggage safely off his head.

"Wow, did you see that *coolie* was carrying four bags," I exclaimed.

"They wear those turbans to evenly distribute the weight," my all-knowing Chettan pointed out, following my gaze.

"I think it's part of their traditional village attire," I responded.

"No, the colour-coding makes it easier to recognise the Coolie association." Shiva, the youngest of the cousins, thought he could correct us both.

"Yes, true. Some people find these red-turbaned luggage-bearers more trustworthy," I chipped in.

"*Chalo* [4] Kamala, Chettan and Shiva," Amma called out, leading us to coach S12. We reached S12 with time to spare. In this 2nd class non-air-conditioned sleeper, each compartment accommodated eight people. On our side of the aisle were two three levelled bunk beds. During the day, the lowest level of these doubled as a bench for three. The middle bunk bed could be folded down to function as a backrest. We always debated about which bed was the best. We found our assigned seats: two lower berths, one upper berth, and one middle bunk bed.

"The top berth is mine," Chettan claimed as he tossed up his luggage. He preferred this one. Sleeping on the middle or lower bed meant he had to get up early, whenever other people woke up. Not me: I loved the middle bunk bed. It felt adventurous. Though, before climbing in, I did ensure thrice the chains were properly latched. The top berth felt dangerous. I was perpetually scared my hair would get caught in the ceiling fan and pull me towards it. The sound of the fan could be quite unnerving. On the top berth I could not sit upright. In the 40C+ oppressive July heat, breeze at the window seat was probably the wisest option, but I did not consider that exciting enough.

---

[4] Come (Hindi)

"Spread out the luggage, Kamala, so no unreserved can sneak in," Chettan insisted. He hated them.

A smile lit up my face, hearing the familiar clang of metal moving on metal. The inertia of the train being overcome, the diesel engine set in motion.

"We're leaving on time, Amma." I pressed my face against the bars of the gated window, trying to spot the smoke exhaled by the locomotive. I could see neither the front nor the tail of the train, so I turned to observe the hubbub on the platform. I watched the *coolies* squatted together in groups. I figured they were taking a breather and a puff before the next travellers arrived. The merchandise sellers jumped off the train and onto the platform as the train gained speed.

We exited the edge of the metropolis, leaving behind the cramped flats, propped up against the tracks. Claustrophobia was giving way. My curls danced with the movement of the train. In the warm breeze I welcomed the open space.

I slipped off my sandals and put my feet on the bench in front. *Chling, kling, chling.* My melodious *payals* jingled as I moved my feet. These anklets were precious to me. The breeze reminded me of the feeling of independence that I had experienced after Amma gave me the anklets to mark my 11th birthday and coming of age. Amma had hung them on my ankles and I had not taken them off since. That day, after all the guests had left, I swayed through the living room on the energetic Mediterranean fusion music of Cirque du Soleil. The door to the balcony was open and in came the monsoon breeze. Finally, a forebode, refreshing rain was on its way. I felt it in every part of my body. Cirque du Soleil's *Alegría:* Joy. Carried along on the operatic tunes, I was gone with the wind.

Lost in thought.

Belgium, India. Two families, so far apart. Family here, family there, family everywhere. Always far away.

After a while I turned around to face my sibling. In a hushed voice Chettan said, "Do you see babyface?"

The people across the aisle had caught his attention, one person in particular. I turned my gaze past Chettan to where he motioned with his eyebrows. Something was strange about the man, though I could not see his face. What was odd I could not figure out. As I was trying to gather as much information as possible, just by staring across the aisle, he turned his head and stared right back.

My eyes shifted and instantaneously focussed on the barren fields with mud huts.

His eyes! His eyes were odd. The colour? The glint? I had not had time to figure out. I wondered how I had sensed this from looking at his back. Babyface, as Chettan nicknamed him, had no resemblance of a baby's face whatsoever. He was a thin-bearded man wearing a prayer skullcap and a traditional sarong-like *lungi*. The name stuck.

"Shall we ask him for a game of *Antaakshari* [5]?" Chettan whispered, winking at me.

I was shaken back to reality and looked at Chettan's eyes. What was it about people's eyes? Ammumma says eyes are the gateway to peoples' souls — and one can easily distinguish between good and evil by looking into someone's eyes. I always wondered how this could be an Indian proverb. In India an unmarried woman is not supposed to look a non-relative male in his eyes. I pulled my nose and eyebrows up in a wrinkle and shook my head from side to side indicating a 'No' to

---

[5] Singing game played in India

Chettan. I was not sure whether we could approach this man; was he good or evil?

"Come, let's sing," Chettan exclaimed. As always he was ignoring my advice.

"Yes, Antaakshari is the best fun pastime for such a long journey," Shiva replied.

Amma pulled the green and white striped cloth bag from under the bench and took out four newspaper packages. "*Chalo* children, come, let us see what Saroj has packed for lunch."

As I pulled up my legs and sat cross-legged with the window as a backrest, Shiva sat facing me, keeping some space in between us on the bench. Amma handed both of us a parcel. I unpacked mine. Folded into the newspaper was a big banana-leaf-package. Dark orange smudges on the leaves revealed the lentil-tumeric-based content. With a smile I dug into my *sambar* rice, with my right eating-hand.

Finishing his food, Shiva burst out in song. "*Aajaa, aai bahaar dil hai beqaraar, o mere raajakumaar tere bin rahaa na jaae...... Aaaaaja!*" We joined him in this first Hindi song starting with the letter A.

"Jaaa, it ends with Jaaa, Kamala it's your turn. Now you sing a song starting with Jaaa."

I hesitated for a moment and then sang: "*Jumma, jumma.....are o jumma, meri janeman, bahar nikal, aaj jumma hai, aaj ka waada he....*" As I was singing I glanced across the aisle at Babyface. Yes, he was watching me. I felt uncomfortable and awkward. Maybe I should have chosen a different song. This Hindi song was about 'Amitabh' asking for a kiss on Friday. It was Friday today. I did not want a kiss. Both Chettan and Shiva, oblivious of the slight frown on my forehead, joined in and tried to imitate Amitabh's coarse voice in the song.

Amma sat near the window reading a book on biotechnology. She was in her own bubble, filtering out any Bollywood influences.

Babyface, dangling his legs over the bench, sat listening to us laugh and sing. He stared into infinity.

Chettan sang, "*Tujhe na dekhu toh chain mujhe aata nahi hai....*"

"*Aadmi musafir hai,*" Amma joined in.

"That's an Aa, Amma. If you want to sing now then you have to start with an ee," I said.

"And by the way. I had not finished, Amma," Chettan reacted.

"Does not matter, it is a nice song," was Amma's response and she continued singing from the 1977 movie Apnapan, describing that people are travellers and they leave behind memories along the way. "*Aadmi musafir hai, aata hai jaata hai, aate jaate raste mein yaadein chhod jaata hai.*"

A soft humming glided over from across the aisle. Babyface.

"*Aap bhi khelna chahte hai?* [6]" Amma asked Babyface whether he wanted to join us. A spark lit up his eyes as he reciprocated the smile.

"*Subhanallah* [7]." He slipped on his sandals and hopped onto our side of the aisle. As he sat down next to me, he brushed his left hand through my hair, patted my head and gave a brief smile to Amma. "*Pyara bacha hai* [8]," looking at me he reinforced this by saying "nice child." Then he looked at Amma and told her about his own daughter who would have been my age today, if she had still been alive. Dengue fever. Compassion in Amma's eyes, a nod from Babyface, unspoken words, life goes on. I realised communication is more than language alone. I felt sorry for him, how he missed his daughter. God works in mysterious ways.

Traffic in the aisle increased as people started preparing for the night. From the opposite side of the aisle a stern grey-haired, Indira Gandhi

---

[6] Would you like to play? (Hindi)

[7] Glory be to God/Allah (Arabic)

[8] Sweet child (Hindi)

look-a-like lady urged Amma to be careful at night. "Bina junction is notorious, you know. They just snatch at anything they can. They do not even enter the train, just from the platform, you know, just like that, just pulling at your jewellery chains and earrings and all. You know, sister, you must be careful. You too sister, you please close the shutters at night. Please all, it is very dangerous." Then looking at me she said, "We stop at Bina around three in the morning, *bacha*. Even the middle-berth is not safe, be careful, you know."

Amma smiled: she wore no jewellery.

Window shutters were lowered, luggage was moved or locked for safety. Berths were latched securely and bed sheets were spread. It was time to call it a day.

"*Chalo* children, go to sleep now."
"Good night, Amma."
"Good night, dear."

I lay in foetus position with my legs facing the aisle. Just to be safe, I took off my *payals* and put them in a small purse which I held on to. I measured the distance from the top of my head to the outer wall and, to be safe, pulled in my head just a bit more.

The whistle of the train. Startled, I woke up and bumped my head against the wall. The train was pulling out of a station. Everyone (except me) was sound asleep, even Indira Gandhi. I needed to know where we were. I realised I was no longer holding on to my purse, it held my treasured anklets and my watch. In the coupe I fumbled for my purse. Amma had not closed the shutter. Where was my purse, had it been snatched!?

On the floor next to Amma's *chappals* [9] a faint light reflected in the beads of my purse. I climbed down and stood on Amma's *chappals*, so as not to get my feet dirty. I picked up my purse to check the contents. It was past three in the morning. The train gained speed. Uttering a sigh of relief, I climbed back to bed.

Next morning, I noticed new occupants in the middle berth and top berth opposite to mine. Traffic in the aisle increased again. People were using the standalone sink and the toilets. The toilets were located near the entrance door, one on each side of the aisle. One western style and one squat. I used the bathroom space out of sheer necessity, and always the squat toilet. The latrine, as the squat toilet was called, had a convenient handle to hold on to during shaky stretches of the journey. These stretches, however, did not justify the perpetually wet toilet floor and human excrement in different nooks and corners of the bathroom. I brushed my teeth and washed my face at the standalone sink, though that too was not the showpiece of cleanliness.

"*Vadeeee, idli, vaddeeee,*" the vendors, clad in khaki coloured shirts, were up early to provide us with freshly prepared South-Indian meals.

After breakfast the middle-aged looking uncle from the opposite middle-berth took out his stash of cards. He tilted his head, looked at Amma, and asked "*theek hai?* [10]" asking her approval to teach us a card game. "It is called Money, children." He looked up at the uncle on the top-berth, "Sir, are you joining too?"

"*Haan bhai*, good time pass *hai.* [11]"

"And you, sir?" he asked, looking at the other top-berth. Chettan did not respond.

---

[9] slippers (Hindi)
[10] Is it okay? (Hindi)
[11] Yes brother, it is a good time pass (Hindi)

The next few hours were spent playing Money and another card game, Rummy. Jokes and laughter filled our coupe, while down the aisle a baby cried and people played Antaakshari. This was all part of the essence of a journey on the Kerala Express.

A refreshing breeze entered through the open windows, teak trees lined the rail tracks. At the next stop, Amla junction, Chettan disembarked, as he did at all stations en route. On this occasion Shiva joined him. I noticed that the majority of male passengers got down to stretch their legs, yet women did not. At most stations the train stopped for a few minutes; at some of the larger stations like Nagpur and Mangalore more time was given.

"Amma, everyone is coming back, I am sure the train is going to leave now. Where is Chettan? I can't see him." I pressed my face against the window bars, "Hey Chettan, *chalo chalo*, come in please."

The train set in motion as Chettan waved at me with a big grin.

"Amma, Amma, Chettan is not coming. Amma, please tell him to come on board." I turned back to look out and saw the intense focus on Chettan's face, his body coming into action as he tried to keep up with the train. He put in a sprint, raised his arm and in a jiffy, with the aid of the door, pulled himself onto the steps of the train. He leaned out, waved a packet of sweet dried-mangoes at us and grinned.

"Chettan, be careful, you give us all a fright, especially your little sister."

"Well, I can't help that she is a *darpok* [12], a coward. I am not, I do whatever I want. Okay?"

---

[12] coward (Hindi)

I took out my summer holiday book: <u>One flew over the cuckoo's nest</u>. Staring out of the window, I was overwhelmed by a feeling of sorrow. Barren mounds specked randomly with bits of blues, greens and whites. Plastic, plastic bags, rubbish. I looked at scattered garbage heaps, instead of a pristine countryside. I wondered whether a single stretch of this train journey did not have plastic or other trash in plain sight. I turned away and buried my head in the cuckoo's nest. I had yet to figure out its location.

"Brrread cutlet, brrread cutlet, nice hot brrread cutlet!" The aroma of breaded deep fried patties dwindled through the air as men and women from the station hopped on the train for a sell. The next announcement followed soon, drowning out the first: "Orange, Fanta, Limca, mango Maaza, cold water. Cold, cold, cold drinks," Each station along the route had its own speciality.

The middle berth uncle had brought home-made lunch. "My wife always adds some extras," he said, passing around the box with potato patties.

Just as Chettan was folding back his newspaper plate, a pantry vendor walked past. "Ice cream, ice cream, vanilla, mango bar, ice crrrreammm."

"Can we have an ice cream, please?" Chettan asked, loud enough so the vendor could hear him.

The vendor, in his khaki coloured shirt and white trouser uniform, gladly stopped and let the heavy ice and ice cream filled metal bucket rest on the side berth.

"*Theek hai*, okay," Amma looked at the ice-cream *wala* [13].

"I want a mango bar."

"Me too."

---

[13] Person, man (Hindi)

"Pistachio for me."

"And one chocolate nuts."

He handed us each our choice.

"45 rupees."

A blanket of midday heat filled the carriage, I pressed my face against the barred window. "I spy with my little eye, a tortoise." I said, looking at the large boulders precariously balancing on top of each other amongst green shrubs and rust-coloured sand covering the soils of the valley.

"Ha, and I spy a sleeping man." Shiva laughed.

"Kamala, close the shutters, let us keep the heat out." Amma said as she stretched her legs, laid her head on the bench, and covered her body with a thin bed sheet. I noticed our co-travellers preparing for their afternoon nap. The swaying motion of the carriage was a welcoming gesture. Embraced by the shimmer of sunrays through the partially closed shutters, I closed my eyes.

The sweeper boy entered, squatting and moving forward like a frog, monotonously sweeping the floor with his 30 cm short broomstick. The boy cleaned under the benches, lifted up shoes but left the bags in place. Unlike many of our co-travellers, instead of throwing it out of the window, I piled up our rubbish in one spot, waiting to be collected by the sweeper. I watched the boy clean the rest of the coupe, no one noticed him. When the boy reached the toilet area, I scuttled back to the window seat.

"Didn't you know they too just throw it out?" was Shiva's response to my look of astonished disappointment.

The scenery changed once again. I caught my first glimpse of the Arabian Sea. Cool refreshing ocean breeze. I buried my head back in the Cuckoo's nest.

"Amma, Mangalore station. Can Chettan go buy some oranges?"

Chettan ignored me, stepped on to the platform and wandered away. A couple of minutes later, his head appeared at our gated window, "Amma, money please." He walked over to one of the many orange vendors at the station. The whistle of the train. The vendor handed a plastic bag with oranges to Chettan. The oranges fell. As the train set in motion, the oranges scattered on the platform. I lost sight of Chettan.

"Amma, we have to STOP the train," I exclaimed, trying to locate the emergency cord.

"Shiva, where is it?"

"There," Shiva pointed at the red box a few seats further down.

I rushed to the entrance.

"Kamala, don't," I heard Amma call.

"But Amma, we lost Chettan."

The train gained momentum, I looked out and saw the station slipping away. "Amma, now what?"

"There he is!" Shiva yelled, as he saw Chettan appear at the end of the corridor connecting to the next coach. He was walking towards us, carrying a plastic bag with oranges.

A sigh.

"Chettan, next time be careful. You give us all a fright, especially...."

"Your little sister."

Today we would reach our summer holiday retreat. Staring out of the window sunk in my own thoughts trying to find the cuckoo's nest, I watched the sun rise through the foliage of coconut and banana trees lining the backwater. Stretching into the distance as far as my eye could see, light-green shoots resembling grass blades were standing in water-clogged fields. Men and women with their feet sunk in the mud, working in the paddy fields. A familiar and comforting sight. We had finally entered Kerala; my fondest — lush green and blue state of India.

During the last lethargic leg of the journey, time passed eating, sleeping, playing Antaakshari and card games again. When Trivandrum Central Station was finally only an hour away, everyone was washed, packed and ready to say farewell. I noticed that bidding goodbyes, in such train compartments, was as easy as forging new friendships for the duration of the journey. Small adventures, on long journeys.

3.
Garden at the Graveyard
The labyrinth and the terrace

Each year we made the trip down South: Shiva, Chettan, Amma and I. Shiva lived with his parents in Delhi, their peak workload was in June. Vijaya lived with Ammumma and Muthachan in Trivandrum. She was almost fifteen years old and was studying and preparing for entrance exams. Her days were filled with tuition classes. She wanted to be a doctor: that does not come easy. Unfortunately, our big break did not coincide as the main recess was in the hottest month of the year; April in the South and June for us in the North.

India, officially one country, but what makes it one country? I contemplated What was the common denominator? I did not know. The contrast between the South and the North was immense. The food, the attitude, the heritage, the languages, all differed greatly. In the South people seemed friendlier, but also more reserved. The two languages, Malayalam and Hindi, did not share the same script. During our stint in Trivandrum, finding the common denominator was one of the topics we vehemently deliberated upon. Chettan focussed on politics, Muthachan on religion, and I pondered on the common trait, the shared characteristics of all. My boundaries went further: I mused on the shared beliefs that connected humanity around the world.

At Trivandrum Central Station, Amma, Chettan, Shiva and I hailed a taxi.

"Please go to the graveyard," was Amma's recurring pre-programmed opening sentence to the taxi drivers, each time we visited Trivandrum. A perplexed look on the driver's face was a perpetual anticipated response.

"Yes, yes, please drive, it is near there only."
"No, Amma, you spoiled the fun," we simultaneously said.

As soon as the vehicle hit the dirt road, we cousins yelled out in unison "Stop".

On the gravel, the slowly moving car came to an abrupt stop. There, to our left, was our summer retreat: a large double-storied recently whitewashed abode amid a multi-coloured labyrinth. The spread out estate, with its many nooks and corners, was an ideal surrounding for crafting new adventures.

When we arrived, Muthachan was waiting at the wrought iron gate to receive us. Formally dressed in trousers and a short-sleeved checked shirt, he was standing at the entrance of the walled enclosure leading to the lush garden. The squeaking gate was a clear signal for Ammumma to emerge from the kitchen and step out onto the veranda. She was dressed in her indoor gown and apron, her hair tucked back in a knot. Vijaya was not home. Tuition or school, I deduced. How much would I see of her this vacation?

As I gave Muthachan a hug, I realised I had grown: I was his height now. Muthachan had also changed. When he patted me on my back, his arms seemed feeble. He had lost weight, and his flagging triceps showed his age. We all hugged Muthachan and stepped onto the veranda. I took off my shoes and embraced Ammumma before entering the house. The kitchen was at the back of the house, and the backyard was Ammumma's domain. Ammumma headed back to the kitchen for the final touches of the lavish banquet she had prepared for us, her guests. It was tradition in Kerala to treat guests as Gods. The first few days in our summer retreat we were considered divine: I did not have to wash my own plate. Vijaya was a member of the household; in a few days I would be, too.

I dropped off my bags in Vijaya's bedroom, which during the holidays we shared. She also used this first floor space for some solitude

32

and intense cramming before exams. Chettan and Shiva shared the ground floor guest room.

During our summer vacation, our daytime routines were all pre-fixed. Everyone knew exactly when and what was expected of him or her. A perfect setting for a quarrel-free stay, but the worst ingredients for an adventurous holiday.

I went to the backyard to see which fruits I could eat today, "Can I pluck a papaya, Ammumma?"

"In the evening, Kamala, papayas should be plucked in the evening."

As I wandered through the vegetable garden, to my dismay I saw a number or *karelas* ready to be tossed in the pan. I knew no other vegetable that was as bitter as this gourd disguised as a cucumber covered with warts. I hoped Ammumma would make the deep-fried version, that at least was edible.

"Be careful, don't walk under the coconut trees," Vijaya came running out to greet me with a bear hug. She had cycled home. Fourteen years old, she no longer wore a skirt, her school uniform had transformed into a *salwar kameez*, a traditional Indian attire.

"Hiiii, so glad you're home already. Nice outfit."

"Yes, from this year on, it's super comfy. I rushed home for lunch."

"And to meet me," I reminded her.

"Yes, that too. Come Ammumma is calling us in." We linked arms, went in through the kitchen and passed Ammumma at the stove. We washed our hands and face and each one of us took to our assigned spot. Ammumma placed a damp banana leaf in front of each of us and spooned a ball of boiled rice on the middle bottom part of the leaf. I took delight in the order of things, each dish had its own specific location on the banana leaf. The mango pickle, coconut chutney and banana chips were placed at the top left corner and we were each given two or three crispy puffed *papadums* to crumble over the *sambar* rice. I added the *ghee*, and saw the butter melt and mingle in the rice. All the other dishes were served in a particular order and placed on specific spots on the leaf. Ammumma had prepared my all-time favourite vegetable dishes: beans *thoran* and mango *pulissery*. I loved chewing the flat mango seed and in the process removing the last bits of succulent flesh as the *pulissery* juices trickled down my throat and chin. I used a ball of rice to wipe my chin dry and popped it in my mouth. Using another rice ball I scooped up the 13 vegetables *aviyal* coconut stew. Licking my fingers when no one watched; what a delight. It tasted DEVINE. Vijaya finished her meal first. I was glad I was a slow eater. Each year I needed a crash course on the protocols of the house near the graveyard. I watched Vijaya fold the top leaf side over the lower leaf side, the other way round was considered disrespectful and was only done at solemn functions. I already looked forward to breakfast: hot crispy home-made *dosas* with coconut chutney.

Once the meal was completed it was time for the obligatory midday nap. Unlike Belgians, Indians do not sunbathe at the hottest hour of the day; instead they nap. Even if I was not feeling tired, I had to follow along and retire to my designated downstairs cot and rest for a while. The anticipation of *chai* and home-made sweet treats is what made the sleepless afternoons during my summer break bearable. Lying in the downstairs bedroom with the summer sun shining on my face I waited, killing the rare mosquito that had found its way into the diligently hermetically sealed off AC section of the house.

After his afternoon siesta, Muthachan came down dressed in his white *lungi* and shirt. This traditional sarong better suited the humid climate. I too had changed into my long pink cotton *pavadai* dress. Chettan wore shorts, Ammumma disapproved. Shiva wore shorts too, that was fine as he was still considered a young boy. Ammumma came down wearing a blue and green *sari*. Her damp salt and peppery waves loosely tied together at the back. Vijaya too had bathed and changed into an airy red and blue *pavadai*. Following our afternoon tea, we were set for the next chore of the day: combing our hair with lice-combs. Even though I had short hair, Ammumma insisted I comb my hair. It was a fun activity and a distraction, especially when I did find lice. The fat ones I detested; when I squeezed them in between my thumbnails the blood spat in all directions. Those ones I preferred to squash on the floor using my comb. The more I combed, the more I scratched, the more I thought I may have lice, the more I combed. A perpetual cycle and perfect entertainment for lazy afternoons. Completing the chore, Vijaya went indoors to finish homework assignments.

In the warm evening breeze, Chettan joined the adults in conversation. Muthachan recalled his freedom fight struggles against the British Raj, and fervently addressed issues in Indian politics. Muthachan and Amma's political views did not match. Chettan loved politics, but found even more pleasure in fuelling heated political discussions on the veranda. I retreated to the utopian garden, where the sweet smell of Jasmine filled the air. Shiva was oblivious to all and dug into The Adventures of the Famous Five, his holiday book for the summer. He brought five books in the series and planned to read them all. I had read many of Enid Blyton's books too, daydreaming of being as brave and tomboyish as Georgina. Everyone wanted to be Georgina, or George as she liked to call herself. Would adventures befall us, as did the famous five? Shiva and I considered Vijaya to be like Julian; the intelligent, caring and responsible kind.

The front garden was Muthachan's domain. A major part of the grounds was a canopy-covered area with sand layering the soil. I walked barefoot, feeling the fine grains wiggle in between my toes, lifting some of them on my feet and kicking them up in the air. I was keen on learning gardening from Muthachan. He knew the names of every blooming flower and flourishing plant. I tried to memorize the names, every summer afresh. Wondering where Muthachan had hung the hammocks this year, I went indoors to get my holiday book. As I approached our room, the door ajar, I heard sobbing. I saw Vijaya sitting at the desk, her back facing the door. I did not go in, I was deterred, I let her be. She too needed space to herself, we had invaded at a stressful moment in her life. She was slogging; all her spare time filled with preparations for Medical entrance exams.

During the next couple of weeks, nothing out of the ordinary happened. Relatives came, had coffee or lunch, chit-chatted with the grownups and then left. Every afternoon we had an obligatory nap. I almost always obliged, willingly or not. The late afternoons I spent either inside the summer retreat or in the garden. In the garden near the graveyard, I was always in search of new structures Muthachan had created or hammocks hung up especially for me. The garden with its secluded patches with a dense canopy covering contained my favourite hideouts for some solitude time. What kept me busy during this summer holiday were my own thoughts. I was not sure whether I would be in India next year nor whether I would visit Ammumma and Muthachan. For work purposes Pa had decided to move back to Belgium and now I had to make up my mind whether I wanted to join him. Here we were being bestowed with love from so many people — blood relatives as well as self-proclaimed family. In India it seems everyone is everyone's family; related by a joined sense of community, caring and sharing. Most of Amma's female friends I called *maasi* [14], meaning mother's sister. They were not really Amma's sisters, but nevertheless they were my *maasis*. Here, we were enveloped in love. I could not bear the thought of Pa all alone in Belgium. We had family in Belgium too, but Belgium was a world apart from India. Belgium was not one big joined family for all. I shed an unseen tear.

Vijaya attended school and was preoccupied, except on Sundays. During the two hour siesta, we had the house to ourselves. The back and front door were bolted and the grounds were off-limits to all. I admit though that we did not always stay put in our rooms. Last year Shiva, Chettan, Vijaya and I had attempted to scale the slanting roof from Muthachan's balcony to the top floor terrace. This terrace was off limits for us children. We had never figured out why, it just was, that's all. Today we were going to give it another try.

Three of us tiptoed up the stairs, past Ammumma's room. We passed Vijaya and Shiva's room. Vijaya was at the desk.

"Vijaya," I whispered. She turned around. "Come join us, we're going up."

When she shook her head and turned back, I spotted sadness in her eyes. Chettan peeked around the corner of the hallway, Muthachan was not around, we presumed he was in his room too. We swiftly turned the corner and scuffled past Muthachan's closed door. Three little mice, with our tails between our legs, we scurried along. Now we had to try to get onto Muthachan's balcony.

"Why don't we go through Muthachan's room instead?" I said, dreading the prospect of having to jump ledges half a meter apart.

"Yes we can try, he usually sleeps like a log," Shiva responded.

"If you wish, *darpok*. You go first and check on him."

---

[14] mother's sister (Hindi)

We retraced our footsteps and reached Muthachan's door. I gently pushed down the handle and softly opened the door. A ray of light illuminated the room, enough for me to see Muthachan, slumbering in his bed. I turned around and nodded at my siblings. I fully opened the door and entered. The last one to enter closed the door. It was dark again. I knew all the nooks and corners of Muthachan's room and I was at ease. Cutting across the length of his bedroom, I unbolted the balcony door and we slipped out.

On the balcony I leaned over and reached for the stiles of the fire escape. I grasped and pulled myself away from the balcony, and gently placed my feet on the rungs then scrambled up the ladder. The boys followed. I reached the overhanging ledge located just a few meters from our final destination. Scrambling up a few arm lengths of the 30 degree slope, I realised this slanting roof would not be the most challenging part of our endeavour. At the top of the slope was another ledge. From here I heaved myself onto the parapet and dropped down on the terrace floor. Shiva needed assistance; I pulled and Chettan pushed.

Up on the forbidden terrace, the midday sun was scorching. Down below in the graveyard, white clad mourners gathered. A common denominator, I realised; both Hindus and Muslims wear white at funerals and conduct the funeral rituals as soon as possible. A difference though: Muslims bury and Hindus cremate their dead.

Concealed by the heat shimmer, I distinguished a white wrapped cotton cloth oriented to the East. I sensed the haziness of this last moment as all were awaiting the deceased's last rites in this world. Perched on this high vantage point I witnessed deep grief and sorrow. Was this the reason the terrace was off-limits?

"I hear a door creak, that must be Ammumma going to the bathroom," Shiva figured. I knew Ammumma's next course of actions.

38

Soon, at the top of the stairs with her candy jar open, she would call my name. How could I get to the bottom of the stairs, as quick as possible?

"Take the fire escape all the way down," Shiva insisted.

"But how do we get there? We'll have to slide down to Muthachan's balcony first."

"And the front and back doors are locked," Chettan added. "Let me go first," he said as he turned around and stepped onto the roof tiles. I followed. My slipper slipped off, it fell on the ledge and tipped over. I heard a thud as it landed somewhere in Ammumma's territory. How to retrieve it was a dilemma to be solved later. I scurried down the ladder, as quickly and carefully as I could. Chettan took the other route, he went to Vijaya's room to instruct her to open the kitchen door for me.

"Kamala," Ammumma called. Catching my breath, I responded at the bottom of the stairs. Ammumma stood at the top with her candy jar open. Vijaya hid in the kitchen. I walked up the steps and took one sweet for each child. I unwrapped the orange one and put it in my mouth, my reward. The banana flavoured one, the least favourite, I decided was for Vijaya. Ammumma went back to her room, while Vijaya tiptoed up the stairs back to her desk.

That summer Ammumma handed down her recipes. During our evening tea she dictated my favourite dishes and I jotted them down in a thin cardboard covered notebook. I intended to cook these with Amma's help, when we were back in Delhi. Although, the chances of that actually occurring were slim. Amma and I were not regulars in the kitchen; Didi's cooking was delicious. Whenever we tried our hands at cooking, it inevitably and perpetually turned out to be a hot and sweaty disaster.

Our month's vacation came to an end, it was time to bid goodbye. Ammumma's goodbyes were hastily conveyed. She preferred to stick to her routines and bestow us with love through food. Later, in her letters to me, she told me how much she missed our company and how empty the house felt without us. "Waiting for your next summer retreat is what I do", she wrote. Muthachan's goodbyes were the opposite. He could not stop hugging us and bid us farewell with a lump in his throat. Muthachan dropped us off at the station. The same story, each year, over and over again.

What did next year have in store for me?

4.
The Belgians
Mon Dieu [15] and the Red Devils

---

[15] Oh my God (in French)

Just turned thirteen, I decided to move back to Belgium. Now I was spending my first summer vacation alone with Pa.

Our plan was a two-week cycling spree in southern France; starting at Aurignac. Pa had done all the preparations and assured me he had chosen a route that would be smooth sailing. Especially the first day would be easy cycling, as "you aren't an experienced *coll* [16]-biker." I had never cycled in hills or mountains. He added, "and we do not want to race against the clock, after all we want to watch the Red Devils defeat the Dutch." Archrivals Belgium and the Netherlands were contesting in the World Cup football match. The Dutch were arrogant and confident they would win, forever recollecting their victorious Orange summer of 1988. Being a one-off champion of European football got to their heads. This year, I knew we, the Red Devils, would put on a brave fight, we would do well. Would we win? I longed to see the game, tomorrow night.

As we reached the bus terminal in Leuven I saw numerous pairs of adults, in cycling gear, waiting near their cars. Surrounded by these cycling pros with fancy multi-geared bicycles, I was David and they were Goliath. I was excited, but apprehensive. Would I manage to conquer a mountain with my six-geared cycle? Two weeks alone with Pa, without any other social distractions, how would I cope?

My grandmother Bomma, Pa's eldest sister and her children came to see us off.

"Danny, catch," my aunt Maria said as she threw him our tent.

"It really is light," she added, "is this all?"

"Yes," I said.

"Every gram counts extra when you need to carry it up a mountain," Pa added.

---

[16] mountain pass (French)

Bomma watched from a distance. A pretty woman with a hairdressers indulgence. Her chestnut coloured bob haircut gave her a typical granny look. Maria was a copy of Bomma, only 20 years younger. As Bomma hugged me and wished me a safe and beautiful journey, I noticed she held on to me longer than usual. I pondered how much she must have missed me, while I lived in Delhi.

"Thank you, Bomma. I will show you all the pictures and tell you the stories when we get back," I said, releasing myself from her grip. When I withdrew, I noticed her moist eyes. They were telling a story, a story I did not entirely grasp.

"Danny, take care of my little girl. I know you want to scale all the *colls*, but please take her abilities into account." I realised Bomma knew Pa well, always challenging his own and others' boundaries.

People had started loading their cycles into the trailer attached to the bus. As I boarded, the driver asked for my ticket. I pointed at Pa. The driver's welcoming nod ushered me in. I entered the stuffy bus and looked at the worn seat covers. Glad that I had decided to wear long trousers, I threw my carry-on in the overhead compartment. The overnight journey would take us to the warm winery roads near Aurignac. At the window seat, I pulled the handle and pushed the backrest back. Then I looked out and blew a flying kiss to Bomma and others. Pa was at the doorstep conversing with the driver, both their eyes fixed on our tickets. He was the last to enter the bus. He took his seat next to mine and said, "Rest well Kamala, we will have some strenuous cycling tomorrow." He took another look at our tickets.

"I hope just only a tiny bit, Pa." I said as I saw my family grow smaller.

"I hope so, Kamala." I heard Pa mutter.

All seats in the bus were occupied. I doubted whether the tight cycling outfits made these grown-ups cycle faster. I figured it only made them look silly. I took out my holiday-read, French Revolutions. It was a hilarious account of the author's attempt to conquer the epic cycling challenge of the Tour de France. Would I be able to conquer our adventure? Pa kept track of the route and kept himself busy mapping out our escapade. Soon the light in the bus was dimmed and I snuggled deep into my seat and closed my eyes.

"Sleep tight, Kamala."

"Good night, Pa."

The wheezing sound of the bus prevented me from falling into a deep slumber. I saw the red digital clock blinking at 5:30. In another three hours, we would reach our drop-off point. I pulled my feet up and lay on my right side. Drawing back the curtain, I peeked out. Sun rays reflected off the bales of hay that lay scattered in the rolling fields. I knew we had long crossed the border, since this was typical French countryside. I closed my eyes again, enjoying the cool morning sun.

6:30 am. The scenery had changed again; brown eroded mountainous peaks on both sides and a couple of stone-cottages dotted the landscape. I looked at Pa and noticed he was bulging over the aisle, arms spread out and an unfolded map in his hands. He was fidgeting. "Ah Kamala, you are awake. Good"

"Good morning, Pa. Did you sleep well?"

"Well, no. I did not want to worry you yesterday, but we are heading to the wrong place."

"What? What do you mean?"

Pa pointed a pencil at Aurignac.

"Yes?" I said. I knew that Aurignac, near the Spanish border, was our drop-off point.

Pa moved his finger across the map moving further up North. His finger stopped in the middle of the '*Massif Central*'.

"Aurillac?" I read out.

"I have a hunch this is where we are going to be dropped off," Pa said.

"Why? What do you mean a hunch?"

"Well, the driver corrected me yesterday. While entering the bus he read out the destination written on our tickets. It was Aurillac and not Aurignac."

"Really?" I was perplexed. How did this happen? I could and should have known, though. My careless dad had done his utmost to prepare well, but accuracy had never been his trademark. Suddenly, I wished I had never agreed to this trip, I knew it was going to be a disaster.

"Aurillac is located in the middle of the mountainous plains of southern France," he said, "I have a gut feeling it is going to be quite a challenge after all. Sorry, Kamala."

"Yeah right." I bit on my lower lip, trying to curb my thoughts from being uttered out loud. Why can holidays with him never be smooth sailing?

Half an hour later the driver announced: "Good morning cyclists. Our first stop is Aurillac. Those of you leaving us, please get ready and be so kind to throw any rubbish you have in the plastic bin bags." After this he added, "The weather seems prefect for some fine pedalling today." Reluctantly I got ready to disembark and collect my cycle from the trailer.

The bus turned right on the single carriageway.

"*Bonjour,*" I said as I gazed at it driving off in the distance. Pa readjusted the luggage. In front of us lay a grassy arid landscape with a number of grey plastered houses and a steep road cutting across. It was Sunday morning, all the shutters were down, most people were probably still in bed. It had the feel of an abandoned hamlet.

"This doesn't seem too bad, 700 meters at an inclination of 7%," Pa read the traffic sign on the windy asphalt road.

I started pedalling and said, "a gentler start would have been better."

Before attempting the ascent, I looked back to check on Pa. He had stopped.

"I think I have a puncture," he called out.

A gentle start indeed. I laid my bike and bum on the roadside. This could take forever. Pa's first task was to patch up the punctured tyre. Luckily he had prepared well for this chore. However, as he filled air in the tyres, I felt my energy was sucked away.

"Come, let us get going. You go ahead and determine the pace, Kamala. I will follow."

I had no choice. Gravel on each side of the road, off we went.

"What's going to be our next challenge, Pa? Dodging oncoming traffic?" I grumbled, out of his audible reach.

Pedalling strenuously, I made it around the first bend. It got tougher as I went through the second bend. I alternated between standing on my pedals and sitting on my saddle. Taking the third bend as my arms started shaking, I gradually realised 700 meters was an exhausting chore in the mountains. A Volkswagen Beetle convertible with two elderly French ladies approached us. I did not want to stop, better to keep the momentum going. As they drove past I heard one of the ladies exclaim

"*Mon Dieu. Ce pauvre petit enfant.* [17]" I understood what they said, so did Pa.

"Pa, we have a problem."

"Yes, I have a feeling it isn't 700 meters after all."

"A zero got rubbed off," I mocked. "How far uphill do you think? I am exhausted." I sighed.

Unaccustomed to cycling in mountains, I disembarked and held on to my cycle while escorting it through the fourth bend, trying not to shake profusely. Then back on my bike, I gradually pedalled around the fifth bend. Alternating between walking and cycling, we finally reached the top of this first peak. My legs were sore, filled with lactic acid. Needles all the way down my calves.

It was time to rest. A picturesque grassy haven, surrounded by brown warn-away mountainous peaks, scattered with patches of green. I lay flat on my back, my legs extended vertically and feet propped up against Pa. He pushed back gently. Pa held on for a few minutes and then released, tenderly bringing my legs back to level ground. Lying on my belly on the green patch, I grabbed a home-made sandwich from the cloth bag. The stale taste was depressing and my mouth was dry. It felt as if I was chewing on cardboard. Pa handed me a chunk of chocolate, expecting it to work miracles.

"Come, time to go."

Reluctantly I stood up and shook off the tiredness from my legs and arms. Vaguely energised, I mounted my cycle again. It was downhill from there. I was in front with Pa following. Uphill had been exhausting. Downhill was nerve-racking. With tense arms holding on to my brakes, I made my way down. Making sure to use both brakes or else I would topple over, so I was told. Adding to the adrenaline was the screeching

---

[17] My God. Poor little child (French)

sound of Pa's brakes, each time he squeezed them. Going downhill, I started paying attention to Pa; was he applying his brakes? I had visions of him flying above my head, being launched from his bike, or skidding past on the asphalt road.

Uphill again, past abandoned farms and then downhill once more. My legs seemed to have found their rhythm, I kept the momentum going. Once in a while I looked up and told myself to enjoy the scenery — the whole purpose of the trip. A few moments of taking in the surroundings were followed by full focus on the road ahead and the momentum of my pedals. Go with the flow.

The hamlet of Sainte Enimie, in the next valley, was a welcoming sight. People on the pavements and shops open. A lively place, not at all abandoned. Pa bought us ice creams in a cone and we walked to the riverbank. The leaves from the trees provided shade. I stretched my legs and took off my shoes, finally time to relax. Paddling my feet in the refreshing stream and licking my creamy strawberry with relish, I looked at Pa. He stared at the unfolded map. He was trying to map our next moves.

"Pa, can't we find a place to stay in this village?" I asked.

"No, no campsites here," he responded.

I knew under these circumstances it was no use arguing with him. I closed my eyes and took pleasure in the intermittent golden shimmers at the back of my eyelids.

"We have to move on Kamala," I heard Pa say. He was at his cycle, ready for departure. I was enjoying our rest — but we had to move on. Reluctantly I got back on my cycle, keeping the Red Devils victory in mind. With a gentle uphill ride we left our picnic spot and headed for our next destination. Pa assured me he thought the next stretch would be less hilly. Finally a levelled road, my muscles could relax. Going with the flow, following the rhythmic movement of my pedals, I continued cycling through French countryside. The wind picked up. I bent over the handlebar and focussed on the road ahead. My body was struggling, I was struggling. Pa, my human windshield sailed past. Now cycling in front, he created eagerly desired smoother waters.

A crossroad.

"Pa, I need food, I can't cycle any further. The ice cream sugars are spent."

"We take a right turn here. That's a restaurant sign, maybe we can pitch up our tent."

"Only if they have a TV, you promised the Red Devils tonight."

It was a Sunday, the café was closed. The proprietor told us to go back to the crossroad and then turn right. She assured me that from the crossroad on, all the way to the campgrounds in the village of Les Visnes, it was downhill. I was not sure whether to trust her information, but I had no choice. Here the TV was inaccessible.

With a slight boost from morsels retrieved from a cookie-vending machine, more dead than alive, we set off on our final stretch.

By the time we entered the stone-cottaged village of Les Visnes, it was 5pm. Grateful to see a campsite sign, it was finally time to rest. The manager smiled as he told us they had ample free lots and we could choose whichever.

We found a neatly maintained grassy spot near the amenities. Because my legs were protesting, I was prepared to walk only the bare necessities. We rested our bikes against the tree, one on each side, and unbuckled the tent from Pa's carrier. As I unpacked the tent, my chest tightened. Frantically I shook out the contents of the pack. Tears welled up. "Pa, where are the tent poles?"

"What?" Pa rushed to my side and went through the parts. A new tent and no poles? A disaster.

"Our camp spot has a lamp post," Pa said, "we can use it to hold up our tent. Let me see what else I can use."

"*Dat soort mensen wil ook gaan kamperen* [18]," I heard someone with a Dutch accent say, as she walked past.

I felt like David again, not up to the task, how would we manage? I heard her conversation partner mockingly reply "they must be Belgians". Her comments made me feel a pariah. Bloody Dutch people I thought, and I looked at Pa. Dutch always made fun of Belgians, but the Dutch were bloody arrogant. I was proud to be Belgian and proud of my 'MacGyvering' father as I saw him skilfully uphold the canvas using the branches of the tree. A helpful camper, carrying an old-fashioned tent pole, walked over to Pa and asked whether he could put it to use. Pa thanked him and set up our home for the night: a tent spun between a lamp post, a tree and a single pole. Not a disaster after all. Campers: a sharing community of like-minded people.

Time for dinner. In the canteen I was glad to see the television tuned to the World Cup football match, though the space was overwhelmingly coloured orange. Orange was the Dutch national team colour, red was ours. I never dressed up in red to watch a game. Most Belgians did not at that time. Dinner was served, my focus was on the game. I barely tasted the overcooked salmon, soggy broccoli and crispy baked potatoes. The game was nerve-racking and the Dutch were loud. Then in the 65th minute, my exuberant Pa and I jumped and cheered. The Red Devil

---

[18] Those kind of people also want to go camping (Dutch)

51

Alberts had scored a goal. In the midst of an orange sea, it seemed we were the only red ones around. No more goals that night. The Red Devils were victorious. I beamed. This was my reward for a hard day's work. The elated red devil in me headed back to our tent.

A thunderstorm was on its way, the manager had warned. I ran back to our shelter, skipping the time-consuming irrelevant brushing of teeth. I wanted to be asleep before the thunderstorm hit. I did not mind the sound, except when thunderclouds loomed ominously overhead and made a cracking noise. Knee-jerking to the lightning flash, I automatically closed my eyes and hunched to make my body smaller.

    A FLASH. I raised my shoulders and crouched. I wanted to hide, but where? I was tense, my neck was one rigid chunk of muscle. Krrr-BAM. I waited for the next flash. This perpetual waiting, involuntarily made my body tenser and tenser.

    "Pa, are you counting?" I asked. I wanted to know how far the storm was. Counting the seconds between a flash and the thunder, I always forgot the maths. The only important thing I remembered was that, if the seconds decreased, then hell was approaching. As a young child in India, one evening I was home all alone and a thunderstorm approached. I was scared for Amma and Chettan who had gone to the open-air bazaar. There was no-one to console me, I hid in a corner, behind the heavy floor-length curtains. There I felt safe. Even now, in my teens, I still needed a place to hide.

    "Kamala, would you like to go to the canteen?" Pa asked.

    ==You think I'm crazy?" I barked, "I am not going anywhere.=="

In the tent I lay on my mat with my head tucked away in my sleeping bag. A towel covering my head, to shut out the lights and smother the sound. As a tiny ball, I fell asleep. Adrift on water.

I opened my eyes and turned to look at Pa.

"Good morning Kamala, glad to see you slept well."

"Good morning, though my body is still stiff. I don't know whether it's from cycling or the thunder. It was really scary last night."

"Yes, lightning has struck five meters from our tent."

"Oh my God," I responded. Now I knew I had not exaggerated my fear of thunderstorms.

"I should have taken you to the canteen yesterday."

"I wouldn't have gone, Pa. I don't go out in a thunderstorm."

"All campers were in the canteen last night."

I rested my hand on the canvas, wanting to sit up. The canvas was soaked. I looked around. The bags were gone. Pa looked at my puzzled face and said, "Yes, everything is wet, everything. It really is a miracle you slept so well."

I had slept through the inundation of our tent. Early morning Pa had emptied the wet bags and had strung a rope between two trees to dry our clothes.

"We are taking it easy today," he said. We had our fair share of adventure, adrenaline and excitement for the whole holiday, all packed into a single day, he explained. "We are going to bike downhill and let the flow of the river guide us to the train station," he said and assured me, "No more struggling in the mountains this summer, Kamala."

That evening a train took us down South. Which new challenges would I face? I wondered and I was curious about what lay ahead. Would I persevere the next time I looked adversity in the face? Would I, or would we, again be able to turn the tables in our advantage, and create a memorable adventure? Things never pan out the way we plan.

5.
A new chapter is written – tabula rasa [19]
Eighteen and carefree

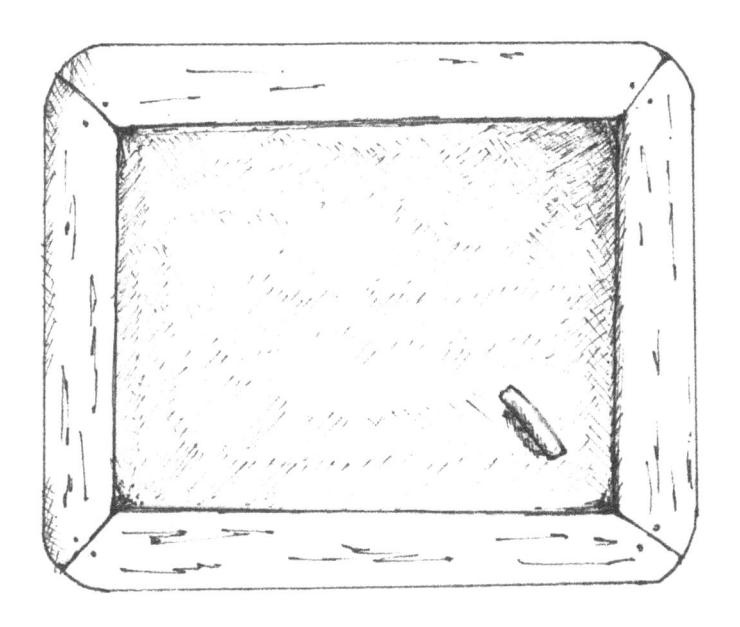

---

[19] A clean slate (Latin)

Adorned with a backpack on my back, a rucksack on my chest, and a sleeping bag tucked under my arm, I approached the balcony of the train where I had safely parked my bicycle. Over the intercom the conductor announced:

"Next station is Wageningen. This train will proceed to Arnhem, with the final destination Nijmegen. If you disembark, remember to take your belongings with you. Have a nice sunny day."

It was Wednesday 1st of September 1999, my first day at University in the Netherlands. A new life awaited me. A milestone, a turning point. I was on the verge of flying out. In later years I understood, many parents find it difficult to embrace this phase. The realisation that their child has grown and creates a whole new world of which they comprise just a tiny part.

In my case, today was a weekday, Pa had to work. Pa was now lecturing in Amsterdam, three years ago we had moved to the Netherlands, to the village of Oostzaan. I made the move to the University town of Wageningen, on my own. I was eager to turn a new page, to start writing a different story. Time had come to live my own life, make my own decisions and be intellectually challenged. I was eager to be among like-minded people. I dearly wanted to spend the next five years of my life, or more, here in this green town. My first acquaintance with Wageningen was a month ago during the Introduction Week. It was a pleasant one, I made many friends. Though intellectually I had not been challenged, sensually I had. The way we danced, in trance, alone in our bubble. I longed to see him again, to get lost in dance, had I met the love of my life?

When I boarded the train, at the unholy hour of 5:45 am, I was astonished by the number of commuters on the platform. The train ride from Oostzaan to Wageningen took around two and a half hours. When I changed trains in Amsterdam, the faint glow of the morning sun emerged through the dark sky. I found a window seat, rested my head on my palm and looked out. Dutch skies have something magical, something mesmerizing, baby pink fluffy clouds loosely stacked and packed together. I was lost in thought in the cotton-wool clouds as they changed shape and colour. Oblivious of the ticking of my watch and the young man's words from across the aisle "you're beautiful".

The conductor's announcement broke the spell.

The train station of Wageningen was a 25 minute bike ride from campus. I unlocked my bike, fastened my sleeping bag and mat on the rear rack, and waited for the train to pull in and the doors to open. I raised my bike onto the platform, then slid it down the stairs and onto the road. My sleeping bag slipped out from under the straps keeping it in place. I stood grounded speculating on how to grab my sleeping bag, hold on to my bike and not tumble over by the weight of my backpack.

"You need help," I heard a voice from behind as I saw a hand pick up my sleeping bag.

"Come, give me your daypack too, I'll fix it to the rear rack," he said.

"But," I replied as I followed his instructions. I did not notice his face, but I knew he was a good Samaritan. I smiled.

Though I followed the signed bike-path to Wageningen campus, it took me longer than I predicted. With only eight minutes to spare, I found the building for my first course: Overview of Inorganic Chemistry. The course was taught not only to Biotechnology students but to all 1st year students studying Life-Sciences. Lecture hall C1000 was in a classical amphitheatre layout, jam-packed with more than 200 students. I walked to the middle aisle and was delighted to see many of my 34 classmates, all of whom I had befriended during our intense Introduction Week. I smiled and waved at the familiar faces in the room, some I had met at one of the many parties and social gatherings, others were friends of friends. Here everyone was someone's friend. Wageningen, a small world. I saw my soulmate too. His unshaven grin made my heart skip a beat. I did not approach him, but instead I slid down to a free spot next to Jessica, pulled down the foldable chair-cum-table and took out my notepad. Shortly after, the teacher entered. Throughout the lecture, I felt his gaze on my neck. Professor Jansen captured my complete attention with his description of chemical reactions. His first and only words to us that morning, apart from bidding us goodbye were:

"Good morning, you fresh batch of students. Pay attention. I do not want to see you in my class next year. Understood." After these words he turned his back on us and started scribbling on the blackboard. I could not comprehend why he made such an odd remark, because all the chemical reactions he jotted down on the blackboard were familiar, I had learned them at secondary school. The only tough part seemed to be to try to keep up with him. He hardly paused while scribbling and as soon as he reached the bottom of the blackboard he picked up the sponge and erased the top part. Towards the end of the class my wrist hurt and I realised that this had not been the exciting start of my academic endeavour that I had longed for.

Three hours down the road, finally a one and a half hour lunch break in which I had to rush downhill to the Haarweg to get the keys to my new dorm-room. The route was a 17 minute straightforward ride. I unlocked my bike, fastened all my luggage and cycled downhill. Soon though, I realised it had been easy riding when I visited Wageningen four weeks ago. I had hitched along with my new friends. I had only seen Wageningen from the rear seat of a bicycle.

I had been biking for 20 minutes and had gone all the way downhill. At the bottom I took a right turn, crossed a busy road, and took a left. I was breathing heavily. Where was I? I must have missed a turn, somewhere. I was LOST. Should I have gone further downhill? I did not know. I assumed it would be straightforward, but now I was stuck in a residential area with no students to ask directions. I biked back to the main road and asked an elderly balding gentleman for directions. Was he an alumnus?

Ten minutes later, covered in sweat, I arrived at the concierge's office. I felt an urge to explain the whole story of how I had got lost and that I was glad I had finally found the place. The look on the concierge's face and his brisk manner made me refrain. I gave him the short version instead.

"Not well prepared for this new life, are you?" he grumbled. "Most students rent their room at least a month upfront." He opened a drawer and took out a long key. "You know the room is unfurnished, right?"

"Yes, I brought a sleeping bag."

"Suit yourself, but that does not seem like a gentle transition," he said while opening a cupboard. It held over 50 sets of keys, each hanging from a nail with a number next to it.

I have already wasted enough time today, so please give me the key and I can leave, I suppressed my inner voice. I twitched my toes and contemplated why I always planned everything last minute and why Pa always wanted to save on money. I appreciated it would have made life easier if I did not have to rush around town today, but then I did not always choose the easy way out, did I?

The concierge gave me the keys to my room and the keys to the common front door of the Haarweg. The Haarweg was a student-accommodation. Its residents were a mix from all walks of university-life: freshmen, recently graduated, PhD-students and postdocs. The Haarweg had a peculiar 1970s architecture. It consisted of three flats, each looked like two crosses joined at the shorter arm. These were separated by green shrubby-grassy patches. Each wing of the cross was a living-unit, called a corridor, which consisted of individual rooms and common-rooms: kitchen, a living-room, toilets and showers. My new address: Haarweg 215 room 219, was located in the second flat on the second floor in corridor number 215. I was glad the concierge took enough time to transfer this crucial information.

I located my corridor, unlocked the front door, and entered a long hallway with artificial lighting. At the far end I noticed bright light; the emergency-exit door. As soon as I entered the hallway the musty smell of laundry hit me and I saw clothes hanging from washing lines on both walls. I also noticed a cubicle with the door left ajar. It had a comfy chair, a ledge with a phone, a phone directory and a sheet of paper hung on the wall with a pen attached to it. Names and numbers were jotted down in various columns. I figured this was a communal telephone booth. Random stuff like an ironing board and an inner drum of a washing machine aligned the walls of the hallway. I looked around and caught a glimpse of a Top Gun poster on my right side and further down the aisle a poster of an unknown movie. Numerous doors opened into this common space, some were open and some were closed. I wanted to drop off my bags and head straight back to class, but the doors were not numbered. I needed help.

A silhouette blocked the natural light at the end of the corridor, leaned back into the room it had just exited, and called, "Hey, we've got company." He turned to me, "Are you looking for someone?"

"Well yes, my room."

"Hey guys, our new housemate." Then turning back to me he said, "Yeah, your room's at the end of the corridor. You've had lunch?"

"Uh, no, not yet."

"Come, join."

I could not resist this offer, though I was running late and had to get back up the hill. It was lunchtime. Fedor invited me to the common living-cum-dining-room, located halfway down the hall. Would it feel like G19? One big joyful family, a bunch of cousins hanging out together? I was curious to find out.

As I entered the bright kitchen area, I noticed two girls seated at the dining table.

"Hi, welcome. I'm Karen. Would you like some bread and cheese?" the slender blond girl asked. She explained how they shared all basic foods and then split the costs at the end of the month.

"Thanks, yes that would be great. I didn't bring lunch. I am Kamala by the way." We shook hands.

"Where's your home-home?"

I was puzzled, a term I had not heard before.

Karen explained, "Where do your parents live?"

"Oostzaan, it's near Amsterdam. It took me 2.5 hours to get here this morning." I gave the easy answer, for now.

"Yes, I know. It takes me 3.5 hours."

"You're at the end of the hallway. I'm jealous, you have one of the best rooms, Kamala. The views are amazing." Paula, the chubby girl, chipped in. In the adjacent living-room two guys were watching TV; 'Cow & Chicken'.

I was going to be part of this HW-215 gang; 14 of us. Seated at the dining table, with the sink at my back I looked at the wall behind Paula.

"Did you paint that?"

"Yes, we did. Well to be precise, Laura did during our yearly spring clean-up weekend."

"Laura is incredible, isn't she? Her room is beautifully painted. When I have an urge to go to the countryside, I visit her room instead. It's amazing what she can do with colours." Karen smiled, "I knock of course."

I looked at the clock in the kitchen, I could not stay much longer. I needed to drop off my bags and head back. I stuffed the last bits of sandwich in my mouth and gulped back a large swish of juice.

The keys fit. I stepped over the threshold of my new home. Two windows on adjacent walls let in vast amounts of sunlight: I was blinded. From one window I had views of the agricultural fields adjoining our building, the other looked out over the courtyard. I paused and gazed out. I could see other windows, windows into the lives of other students. I felt privileged to be part of this community. Over time, I would often decide to keep the curtains of the second window drawn. Not everyone needed a peek into my life.

In the late afternoon, as I opened the door to my 18m^2 barren room, again I was greeted by sunlight and the room felt like home. Finally alone, after a full day of lectures and laboratory work, I unpacked my bag. Clothes, shoes, a radio-alarm clock, a sleeping bag and mat: all basic necessities for a week-long camping in my own room. Next Sunday Pa would drive over with my furniture and other belongings. Seated on my mat, with my back resting against the wall without a window, I noticed the walls were well maintained and I pondered on the effect of the soft yellow colour. Would it liven up the room on gloomy days? Today it bathed me in a warm glow of yellowness.

I had my own sink. I washed my face with warm water. Welcome home. I opened my diary to the first blank page and started writing.

Wednesday 1st Sept '99

Dear Lei,

I am going to write here dutifully, every day! My first day in my new hometown Wageningen, and already I have so much to tell. Our Biotech group is really awesome. It's really easy to get to know each other real quick. Just 34 of us. I already know everyone's name and where they're from. It's also amazing how there seems to be a click straight away, with everyone. And yes, the chemistry was definitely still there, when we met today! We didn't say much to each other, but I feel it, the mutual connection. It feels awesome!

My housemates seem super chill too. ==Well maybe not all of them, I still haven't met all ;).== The ones I met at lunch: Karen, Paula and Fedor are cool, although...

I heard a knock on my door.

"Yes?" I opened the door.

"Are you joining us for dinner?" Karen asked "Do you want to help cook, then you don't have to do the dishes."

"Oh, yeah, great, sure," I responded with a grin matching hers. After dinner while the others were doing the dishes, Karen asked whether I wanted to join in playing the game 'Settlers of Catan'. Jeroen stopped his washing duty and said, "Yes, we do need a fourth player."

"Since when do you join in Catan, Jeroen?" Fedor shouted from across the living room, mingled with Chicken's voice.

"Always in need of a female player," Jeroen added, bursting out in a deep hearty laugh.

I could not resist.

After Paula became the trader with the longest trading route, the game ended and we moved to the living room and were lost in conversation till the early hours of Thursday. The beer fridge with registration sheet was close at hand. Payment would be settled at the end of the month, together with payment for breakfast, dinner, toilet paper and phone calls. Jeroen walked over to grab another round of beers. "Hey, there is Marc. Fedor come have a look, you'll enjoy this," he said in a jolly tone. A belly laugh followed.

We all went to the full length windows. In a room in the opposite building, no curtains, two naked bodies entangled.

"Uhh, uhh, uhh, yeaah" Jeroen shouted out, followed by a rhythmic "Yes, yes, yessss!"

"Hey cut the crap, Jeroen, by the way he lives on the 5th floor, they're on the 7th."

Jeroen turned around and winked at me, "Be careful what you do in your room, lovely Kamala." He walked to the hallway, "I am leaving, ladies. Uh, uhh, uhhhhgh." A bouldering laugh.

Next morning, long before my radio switched to the 8 o'clock news, I realised the need for curtains. I put on sweatpants and entered the hallway. I strolled through the hallway, worried I might walk into someone's bedroom. There was no missing the bathrooms though, these were cubicles partially protruding into the hallway. I counted three bathrooms and three toilets. The toilet with pinups of Pamela Anderson seemed off limits for me. It also felt filthy. I preferred the one with pinups of Tom Cruise and Johnny Depp — or the one decorated with posters of international works of art. The warm strong shower had awakened me and I went to the dining room. Karen, Fedor, Jeroen and a guy I had not yet met were having breakfast.

"Good morning, bright and early rise, sunshine."

"As I say, man it up in the evening, man it up in the morning."

"Yes, I never miss a class," Karen acknowledged.

"Our knight in shining armour is of course still fast asleep."

I took a bowl from the cupboard, then grabbed granola and milk from the table.

"Hey look, a bird!" Karen's boyfriend remarked.

"What?"

"Yeah, it just plunged down. Didn't anyone see it?"

We all let out a bouldering laugh.

Thursday's class was similar to Wednesday's, except for the laboratory class in the afternoon. It had made me famous, or perhaps infamous. Pressing the red button, I shut down the energy supply to ¼ of my classmates' lab setups. The steam explosions emerging from my system set off all my alarm bells and involuntary turned on all the panic switches in my body. I lunged forward and hit the red button. The RED button, to be used in case of emergency, the lab assistant instructed us at the start of the class. Had it been an emergency?

On Thursday evening when I came home past midnight, I popped into the living room to grab a glass of milk. From the corner of my eyes I saw my Nigerian housemate Kalela dozed off in a comfy chair. I could only see his face, not the rest of his body. The TV was on and the sounds it was producing were explicit. I did not have the inclination to watch, yet I did not turn it off either. Was he watching porn in the living room? I felt embarrassed. However, I could not stop my mind from wandering, recollecting the vibe of the evening in my sensual bubble with John. Next morning the television was off, my visuals remained.

My first week in Wageningen flew past like clouds. It was Friday and I was on my way to home-home. In the train, on the last stretch from Amsterdam to Oostzaan, I opened my diary.

Friday 3rd Sept '99

I intended to write here daily, I didn't succeed, did I? So many things I want to write, so many new experiences, so much happening. But when to write?! I have no time!

Wow, I am so glad I am here in Wageningen :-). I feel so at home and it's amazing how easily I can make friends here. It's already Friday now and I'm on my way home. Pa will want to hear all my stories too. Though some I think I'll keep to myself ;-). ==Will he disapprove of the lack of hours of sleep and that we played games till the early hours of Thursday morning?== *At Thursday night's party he probably thinks I drank too much, maybe I did, but I* didn't skip any class the next day. I have to discover the world on my own, in my own manner. Falling and getting up and maybe falling again. He's been a student too, he must understand. We have never talked about this before, maybe this weekend I will use the opportunity to ask him about HIS student life.

My classmates are so vocally apt. I often seem to get overruled. I'm in admiration of how they start all these interesting new conversation topics and throw in amazing facts and figures. I do feel a bit dumb in this abundance of cleverness and blatant self-confidence. ==I do think I've made myself infamous by pressing the RED button!== Well come think of it, not everyone is vocally overpowering. Jessica is clever too, but she is soft-spoken. Maybe I can be more like her, articulate my thoughts well-structured. Make people listen. I hope I will do well; I hope I belong here. But for now I'll just enjoy myself.

Classes haven't been a real challenge yet. I guess these first few weeks will just be a recap of what we learned in secondary school, that's a shame. I want to be challenged. Though with less than six hours of sleep, maybe it's not that bad after all.... Emotionally, it's a different story. I am feeling confused. At the party yesterday we danced again, the way we did a month ago, bodies almost touching, a thin silver elastic in between us, pulling and pushing. We were lost in each other and shielded in our own little world, then I had to pee. When I came back from the loo and went to get a drink, Sandra was at the bar too. "Do you know John has a girlfriend back home?" she said. I can't believe this, IMPOSSIBLE! The way we dance, it definitely means something more than just dancing. I can't believe he is committed at home-home! Is my imagination playing tricks on my heart and soul? I thought I had met my soulmate. Have I? Haven't I? So...oh bugger, need to wrap up, my train is pulling in. Well hope to find out soon!

Love,
Kammy

6.
Magical Machu Picchu
A Sol [20] for your thoughts

---

[20] Peruvian currency

What made me come to this part of the world? I do not know. I suppose it was not a well weighted decision. I was following my heart's desire. In my teenage years I had felt an urge to travel to South America. In Belgium and the Netherlands, many considered me too exuberant. I had heard *Latinas* [21] are spirited. I wanted to blend in, I wanted to be a Latina. What triggered it, I do not know. A cultural chameleon longing for new colours? After passing my first-year 'propedeuse' degree, I took a year off from student life. I spent six months cleaning university buildings to top up my bank account for future endeavours and (ad)ventures and now here I was. I was in Peru, my first venture abroad.

Two months ago, the long haul across the Atlantic Ocean brought me to a world that felt familiar yet unknown: Lima. My plane landed at 7pm, I was tired, it was dark. Anxiously in search of a familiar sign at Arrivals, I spotted a board with:

Bienvenido [22] *Kamla*

"*Hola, Gracias,*" I said as I put my red North Face 60 litre backpack in the back seat, and I joined the driver in the front seat. I felt an unease. The area we were driving through resembled a slum in Delhi. Narrow streets, people and children sitting in front of flimsy houses and scooters overtaking us left and right. It was too dark for me to distinguish between the open gutter and the road. Tea stalls and corner shops lined the street. I wished the driver would keep pace and not slow down. I did not know how to lock the door from the inside. I prayed no one would pull it open and grab me or my belongings.

"*El otro camino tiene mucho tráfico* [23]," he said, probably in response to my unease at this unusual route. Fortunately my crash course

---

[21] A woman from Latin America (Spanish)
[22] Welcome (Spanish)

Español helped me understand that the other route was congested. By the time we reached the hotel, I was exhausted. The surroundings of the hotel felt familiar; an Indian middle class colony. Small fenced off gardens and courtyards with two storied buildings. The security guard on duty gave me a welcoming grin, making me feel at home. My tiredness seemed to slip away.

The next morning I was greeted by *señora* Vic from the organisation Mundo Saludable. The coming two months I was going to help out at this NGO in a village in the Cordillera Blanca mountain range. I would live and travel off the beaten track in Andean Carhuaz. Here, submerged in *Español* I learned to swim: *nadar* [24]. In my second week in Carhuaz, during an outdoor fiesta, a woman, whom I had not met before, handed me her infant and went to a stall to buy some food. I marvelled at the realisation that here I could easily blend in. At that moment I was a Latina, as long as I kept my mouth shut. My dark hair and mixed race complexion made me look local. The only other English speaker in this village was an elderly gentleman *señor* Anthony. For me, Anthony embodied a welcoming weekly relaxation moment. After two months my fluency in Spanish improved and it was time to move on. It was time to go on new adventures, to spread my wings and fly. Time to transform into a backpacker.

    I did not want to be a tourist, not to be one of the flock. A traveller, yes. A tourist, no.

However a tourist I was, as I headed to the touristic epicentre of the South American continent. In Cusco I stayed in hostel Albergue Municipal, a clean white colonial style building with friendly young

---

[23] The other road has a lot of traffic (Spanish)
[24] To swim (Spanish)

Peruvian staff. Friends in Carhuaz had warned me of altitude sickness and had given me ample advice. These I put into action. The first four days I spent acclimatising to the 3400 meters above sea level, sipping on coca tea and exploring the streets *como una latina, despacito* [25], slowly. Taking my time to observe anything and everything: soaking up this new culture. This culture, where both the Catholic Church and the Earth Goddess '*Pachamama*' played an important role, fascinated me. Reclining on a sun warmed stone structure at the Plaza de Armas, watching tourists and locals, again I wondered, do I blend in? An occasional "*De donde eres?* [26]", where are you from, resulted in entertaining and enjoyable conversations. My response was "*De donde pienses?* [27]" wanting to know what they thought. Was I Argentinean, Chilean, Ecuadorian or even Peruvian? These were countries I still planned to visit. I was glad no one had yet called me a *gringa,* a disparaging slang for American woman.

The first few days in Cusco I tried arranging a trek that did not go directly to the famous Machu Picchu. All backpackers went to Machu Picchu, but walking in file up those ancient steps to me seemed like a drudge. It seemed like a tiresome chore, definitely not an adventure. I did not feel inclined to tread up the Inca-Trail to the Sun Gate for a first sunrise glimpse of this world wonder, if it included hundreds of others. It was off-season though, so there were not many treks being offered. It turned out to be quite tough to book anything but the Inca-Trail. I dropped by the travel agent each day, but by the fourth day I had not been able to book an alternative trek. I felt disappointed and was distressed. As a last resort, I decided to book the Inca-Trail first thing the next morning.

---

[25] like a latina, slowly (Spanish)
[26] Where are you from? (Spanish)
[27] Where do you think I am from? (Spanish)

That evening at 7 pm the travel agency called Albergue hostel.

"Si, Kamala?"

"Yes, Si."

"Tomorrow morning at 5 the group is leaving for the Salkantay trek, you can join?"

Luck was on my side. The Salkantay trek went to Machu Picchu, but the trail had no historic significance. It was recently 'discovered' and opened to the public. I expected it would be less crowded compared to the world famous Inca Trail.

"Si, *seguro* [28]," was my response and I started repacking. My backpack was heavy. During my travels I had days that my shoulders ached. I wondered: why did I always lug around so many belongings? There and then, I made a decision: next time I would reduce some of the bits and pieces I carried along. On tomorrow's trail I would have to carry my own bag uphill, therefore the lighter the better. I left my 60 litre backpack in the storage room and packed the essentials for a four-day Salkantay trek to the thermal springs of Aguas Calientes and the world-wonder Machu Picchu. I followed the advice of Violeta, a girl working at the hostel. I took along 100 sol, the rest of my money I left stashed in my red backpack. We both figured this would suffice for the duration of the trip since lodging and transport were included in the trip and already paid for. I stashed an extra $10 in the sole of my right shoe, just in case.

At dawn I quietly got ready and left my fellow snoring backpackers asleep in their bunk beds. I was eager for new adventures to unfold.

I waited at the massive round wooden front door. There he was, Jorge, a good-looking slim-build Peruvian with Chinese features. He seemed *simpatico* [29]. As we walked through the lantern-lit streets of

---

[28] Yes, sure (Spanish)
[29] pleasant male (Spanish)

Cusco, Jorge and I talked in Spanish. Jorge spoke English, but I loved conversing in my new *lingua*[30] and I realised that Jorge felt more comfortable in Spanish. I contemplated whether a conversation in one's mother tongue is more intimate.

In total we would be six in the group; four guys, me and another girl from Austria. At the next hostel there was no-one waiting to be picked up. The door remained closed even after Jorge rang the bell thrice. The four guys were not going to join us after all. Possibly snoring through their hangover, I thought. People are *loco* [31], they come all the way to Peru, just to drink booze and sleep in. What a shame. I was glad they had booked the tour the previous day, or else it would have been cancelled with just two trekkers. I doubted whether I had made the right choice after all. Should I have opted for the Inca-Trail instead? I counted myself lucky though that Kim had decided to join. She could have cancelled last minute due to her injured knee. I wondered how she would manage to keep up with us, well, with me. She was not going to do any strenuous walking.

As we boarded the local bus that would take us to Sallapata, which was the starting point of our trek, I scanned the seats. I saw no other *touristas*, only Peruvians. Then two *gringos* and a Peruvian entered.

"*Hola*."

"*Hola*," we smiled at each other. The boys strolled to the back. I was excited and curious to know where they were heading, perhaps we had the same objective in mind?

After a three hour drive all *gringos* and their guides disembarked.

"Doing the Salkantay trek too?"

---

[30] Language/tongue
[31] crazy (Spanish)

"Yep."

"Have fun and probably see you later." I waved at them as they set out on their hike.

Two grey-coloured slender, fit looking horses, their carer and a cook were waiting for us. The boys, Josh and Peter, left with their guide Jesus. I had assumed we would follow them, but Jorge led us in the opposite direction.

"That's a shame," I looked at Kim, as we followed our guide to a path leading uphill to the Vilcabamba mountain range.

"Yes, I would rather take the other route," she murmured, "less uphill."

Halfway up the first hill we stopped for a breather. Green pastures surrounded us. As I turned around scanned the other hill, I saw them pausing too. Specks on a green slope, they looked lost. Jorge waved at them. Their guide waved back and then turned around to face the boys. They turned and retracted their footsteps. Before long, they hiked up the narrow rocky path in our footsteps. Soon they caught up with our slow group, as Kim was walking. One of the horses was equipped to transport Kim whenever needed, but she insisted on walking a while.

"What happened?"

"Jesus isn't our saviour after all," Josh replied mockingly.

"Jesus took the wrong route."

"Really?"

"Yes, crazy," Peter replied, his lips pressed together and his eyebrows slightly raised.

"I think we are joining you girls," Josh winked at me.

"Great, the more the merrier," I responded.

"Quite bizarre, our group. Four trekkers, three horses, a cook, a horse-carer," Kim chipped in, "and two guides" gesturing quotation marks as she said the last word.

"Yeah, what happened to the other trekkers in your group?" I looked at Josh.

I tried figuring out where they were from. I guessed they were in their mid-twenties. Tall men with dark-blond hair, I would not call either good-looking. Though Josh caught my attention, something about him made me prone to liking him. The four hour gradual climb to our first resting spot gave us ample time to get to know each other. The warmth of the sun and intermittent cool breeze were welcoming companions on the non-strenuous ascent. Joking and laughing throughout the uphill walk, Josh and Peter made fun of Jesus whenever possible. Josh, the tallest of the duo, would run up to Jesus and abruptly stop just before crashing into him. Then, Peter in a high-pitched voice would exclaim "Jesus, where do we go now?" Whenever the path forked off in two or more directions, the same high-pitched voice, posing the same question over and over again. Jesus seemed to take the jokes lightheartedly, a grin appeared on his face and he punched the boys away. On other occasions he seemed to ignore them. I wondered whether Jesus was pleased with his 'customers'. I smiled at my new companions, two goofy 'Kiwis'.

By 5pm we reached our destination for the night. Barren, windswept Salkantaypampa, nestled at the base of the majestic Andean snow-covered peaks. As soon as we reached this *pampa,* the cooks got the fire started for a *pollo saltado*. This backpacker's staple food was a Peruvian style chicken stir-fry with onions, bell peppers, and potatoes.

"We have two tents for you. One for the girls and one for the boys. Not for fun," Jorge winked at Josh, "but for sleep. You will need energy tomorrow." He put the camping gear on the barren soil, ready for us to set up.

"Tea is ready," Jesus said, "first drink warm tea." I readily agreed. The Kiwis first drink of choice was not available, they settled for second best.

Setting up the tents was a piece of cake, after which it was time to relax. I was famished and ready to attack the chicken stir-fry as soon as it was served. I sat cross-legged on the mat Jesus spread out on the ground. The chicken was well prepared and the vegetables had a bite to them. It tasted delicious, maybe the best stir-fry ever. The agreeable company, the uphill climb, and the pampa air had a positive appetizing effect.

"There, look, Mount Salkantay," Jorge pointed at the glacier-capped summit straight ahead. "The Incas worship it. It means Wild Mountain in the local Quechuan language. We will go there tomorrow." The next day would be tough, Jorge warned us. "Good night amigos. Sleep well."

We got ourselves ready for that first night on the pampa. I had NOT prepared well. At midnight, I hunched up in my sleeping bag and groped through the rucksack in search of warmer clothes. I wished I had brought my red backpack instead: it held more clothes. I was already wearing a long sleeved black coloured shirt and matching stretch trousers. That was not doing the trick, so I put on another long-sleeved green shirt, red tracksuit trousers, black woollen socks and a blue fleece sweater. Rainbowed, I cocooned back into my mummy-sleeping bag, all zipped up. A sleeping bag bought in a market in a Northern Peruvian town, meant to keep me warm and comfortable at 4 degrees Celsius. Here on the freezing *pampa* I realised I had been ripped off. These individual clothes in themselves were not warm, but together they would create an extra isolation layer. My hope of feeling snugly warm unfortunately turned out to be too optimistic. Lying in a double layer of clothes, I wondered what I would wear the next day. Removing one set of clothes and wearing my rain-and-windproof Gore-Tex down jacket would hopefully do the trick. I envied Kim, sound asleep.

I woke up early. A restless night. I did not feel my usual bubbly self. At breakfast I saw sleepy eyed faces. Would a shot of caffeine do the trick for us? After a heavy breakfast of porridge and coffee I felt energized and looked forward to another day on the move with enjoyable people. The first part of the climb today was another gradual ascent. We passed a shallow grey lake, which looked like a puddle when viewed from the top of the hill. Before long we tread on the gravel of the Seven Snakes, the so called zigzagging path of the 'Siete Culebras'. It was an abrupt ascent to a height of 4700 meters. The scenery changed to rocky hills, yesterday's green pastures were long forgotten. As we clambered up the slope, mist came crawling towards us. A mystical vibe filled the Salkantay pass as the fog swirled around us. We stepped carefully, visibility diminishing to only an arm's length. As we strode through the haze I spotted cairns scattered all around.

"Fascinating how the same practices have emerged across the world." I said, after explaining cairns in the UK to Jorge, an offer to the Gods for a safe passage.

A photo-moment as Kim and I built a little cairn of our own, placing different sized stones one on top of the other. Photobombed by the Kiwis. From that moment onward, it was all downhill. It felt lovely to leave behind the chilly Salkantay pass and move on to warmer weather. It was a dramatic change. The lush green cloud forests welcomed us and seduced me into removing one piece of clothing after the other. The trickling streams turned to wild waterfalls and broad currents.

"I'm afraid of heights," I explained, as I made my way across a logs-and-rope river crossing. I had barely uttered these words, which were lost in thin air, when I felt the bridge sway. I was stuck between the Kiwis, Peter walking in front and Josh behind me. The bridge was swaying again.

"Guys, please," I stammered.

"I am here. Holding your back," I felt Josh's firm hands on my shoulders and his chin on my head. "You're in good hands, *chica* [32]," he whispered in my ear. "Good to go, Peter," Josh called out. "Wooosh, woosh, woosh," we continued walking forward as Josh made the sound of wind while holding me firmly. His warm breath softly brushing past and caressing my cheek. Peter, unaware, continued swaying the bridge.

We reached La Playa, which is Spanish for 'the beach'. Why it was called the beach I could not understand. There was no sea nor lake, only a sandy riverbank. This sandy strip did not stop us from stripping and plunging into the icy cold river. The dip was refreshing, but something only *loco gringos* would do. Maybe it is something only *loco* Kiwis would do, or just any Kiwi? All Kiwis are crazy. A smile crossed my face, was I a Kiwi too?

The final day was laid back. We spent most of the day in the back of an open truck. At the village of Santa Teresa we disembarked and crossed the river in a cable-cart, fit for one person. On the other side a truck drove us, and local Peruvians, from Hydro-electrica to a railway track that would lead us to our final destination of 'Aguas Calientes' village. We only walked for two hours that day. Kiwiness rubbed off. We outperformed each other with circus acts, and tight-rope walking the last stretch of the tracks.

"Kamala, you can't come all the way to Aguas Calientes village and not go to Machu Picchu. You're almost there."

---

[32] Girl, chic (Spanish)

"But I have no money on me, Josh."

"We told you, we can lend you. We have enough," Peter tried persuading me.

"We'll get a new train ticket for you too, tomorrow, Jesus has ours," Josh added.

I did not need much persuading. I accepted the offer of borrowing money for the entrance to Machu Picchu. I enjoyed their company too much. I did not want to bid goodbye yet.

Wanting to avoid the hordes of tourists, we decided to visit the ruins in the late afternoon. The following day as we walked the steep path up the hill from the village to the entrance of the tourist site, I became aware of my own insignificance. Walking uphill I could not yet catch a glimpse of this world famous Incan miracle tucked away on a platform surrounded by the high peaks of the Vilcabamba. I pondered on how the Incas built this settlement on a mountain ridge and how this abandoned city was discovered by an American more than 300 years later.

As I set foot on sacred ground, I was mesmerized. There it was. The breathtaking Sacred city: A man with a long nose. Lying on my left hip, my head resting on my left hand, I took in the face-silhouette view of this old civilization of Machu Picchu. Such serenity. I tilted my head up to receive the warmth of the sun.

I wandered through the ancient stone-rooms of this ruined citadel on my own and marvelled at the ingenuity of these Incan structures. In awe with how perfectly well these individually carved stones fit one on top of the other, without the use of mortar. As I strolled past, tapping at the joints and stroking the stones, I was grateful my stubbornness for deterring from the trodden Inca-Trail had not deprived me of this sublime experience. Glad we had opted for an afternoon visit I wondered how it had felt for the American archaeologist Bingham when he first set eyes on the lost city of Machu Picchu, in 1911 still untouched by inquisitive humans. Today I was exploring. The intricate network of stone terraces seemed deserted. The varied coloured orchids perched upon the stone structures struck a sensual chord. I had never before noticed that flowers could be this graceful. Josh brushed past. I blushed.

Past sunset, we returned to Aguas Calientes village, exhausted.

"Kamala, we're staying one more night," Peter told me. They needed time to relax in the hot springs, he said. Kim left by evening train back to Cusco. "No plans, just soak in the Aguas Calientes tomorrow, then we've seen it all, done it all."

"I have no money on me, guys." The 100 Sol I had brought along on the trip exchanged hands when I said goodbye to the cook, porter and guide.

"Don't worry, *chica*. We'll be fine. We can share a room," Josh said, as a mischievous smile crossed his face.

I was dependent on them. Without my own means nor money, I was at their mercy. I had to follow. I wondered: would I have made a different choice if I had been alone and listened to my mind instead of given in to this rush? This tingling sensation was getting a grip on me.

Once in the hot springs, I felt my muscles rest in the warmth of the natural warm water. It was soothing. A great decision after all.

"We can't find Jesus," Peter said when we were back in the hotel.
"Bastard, he left without giving us our train tickets."
"Damn."

There we stood, the three of us, on the cobblestones. Stuck in this humid magical place with hardly any money to spare. Trapped. The only way to leave this tourist trap was to take the expensive train — or walk. No cheap bus options and no cash machines available. No money to get us out of here. I sighed.

"Let's have an ice cream, mate," Peter suggested.

"What flavours do you want, Kamala?" gentleman Josh asked me.

"Thanks, I am okay." I could feel the pinch.

I waited outside the ice cream parlour while the boys stood in line. Did I hear coins fall? My eyes frantically scrutinized the pavement. Oh my God, how deep can one sink? The attitude of *mañana mañana* [33] or 'we'll see what to do when it hits us', was a life lesson I still needed to learn.

On the 5th day, contrary to my original plan, we started our 10 km walk back to Hydro-electrica along the railway tracks. This time I was apprehensive. It felt unsafe to walk through a tunnel without a guide. Yet all went well. After passing through the tunnel we reached the end of this first part of our adventure, our trip out of Machu Picchu. Foolishly, I expected to see a truck, this time though no truck awaited us. The only vehicle I saw was a garbage truck which was overloaded with garbage and boys sitting on top. It started raining. I dearly wanted to get out of this place.

"*Señor, puedes llevar nos a* Santa Teresa? [34]" I asked the driver for a lift. We managed to squeeze ourselves in the front seat of the garbage truck, three of us and the driver. Squashed in between Peter and Josh. On each bump I felt Josh's fingers tickle my shoulder. It was a bumpy — and ticklish — road.

---

[33] tomorrow, tomorrow (Spanish)
[34] Sir, could you take us to Santa Teresa? (Spanish)

"*Pobrecitos, tienen que sentar se en la basura* [35]," I exclaimed, looking at the driver and feeling pity for the boys sitting on top of the rubbish, in the downpour.

"*No importa* [36]," he replied, it seemed they were used to such conditions. They would shower once they got home, the driver reassured me. Our bags did not fit in the cabin and joined the boys on the truck in the pelting rain, under a sheet of plastic.

The garbage truck dropped us at the gorge and the dingy cable-cart across from the village of Santa Teresa. We needed to cross the river. While going to Machu Picchu village, each of us used a separate cart. This time, however, Josh joined mine. The cart was not made for two *gringos*, I wondered whether two locals would fit in. I sat in the cart, Josh's legs engulfed mine as he tried squeezing in. Our bodies were pressed together, I could feel his heartbeat and his muscular chest pressing against my back. I held on to the carriage, he held on to the ropes. The ride was short, the sensation lingered on.

When we got to the village of Santa Teresa, I hoped we could catch a bus to Cusco, using the little money we had left.

"*No hay bus ahora* [37]," we were told by the *señor* at the restaurant. He offered us fruit juice. The next bus was scheduled to leave at 3am. *Probrecitos* [38]*!*

"We do not have enough money to rent a room."

"Not even enough to rent just <u>one</u> room," Josh stressed on the number and looked at me. I could feel the chemistry growing stronger.

---

[35] Poor chaps, have to sit on the garbage (Spanish)
[36] Does not matter (Spanish)
[37] There is no bus now (Spanish)
[38] Poor buggers (Spanish)

The *señor* was heart-warmingly friendly, he allowed us to sleep in the restaurant after the last paying customers left. He swept the floor, and the tables and chairs were set to one side. It was a restaurant not a hotel, but there was enough space for us to roll out our sleeping mats and have a rest. My mind wandered, Oxytocin kept me awake.

At 5am sitting in the bus I felt a sigh of relief, finally we were on our final stretch out of Machu Picchu, magical Machu Picchu.

Then the bus broke down.

Was my wish being granted, a way of spending more time with this bloke?

Sitting on the roadside, I took off my shoes and remembered. I turned my back to the others and removed the sole of my shoe. Paper. I unfolded it. Aha, yes, the hidden $10 US dollar bill. I wondered whether anyone would accept this sod of paper. It smelt mushy and was soggy. I tucked it into a side pocket of my rucksack and walked to Josh, kicking at some pebbles. Unspoken words, I did not know what to say, I longed to be near him. I twirled a strand of hair between my fingers.

One and a half hours later, back in Cusco, the moment I was dreading had arrived. It was time to say, hug or maybe kiss goodbye. It was an endless hug, our bodies glued together. Would I ever see him again? Our arms in search of the right spot to rest for this much desired embrace. Then he fondly held my hips and gently pushed them away from his, creating some distance.

"Have fun, *chica*, it was lovely getting to know you," he said jolly affectionately.

Strangers again, backpackers, each on our own personal quest.

Back at my hostel, my mind wandered again. I retrieved my rucksack from the storage space, but I did not check the contents. Are all my personal belongings still in place? Should have been the question I asked myself. Is fate playing games with me? Was the question on my mind. Violeta told me the hostel was 'fully booked'. This undeniably is providence, I thought. I rushed to Josh's guesthouse just a few minutes down the road. As I opened the gate and stepped into their yard, I saw the boys. I saw the twinkle in his eyes. My heart skipped another beat. The owner was kind enough to add a bed to the boys' spacious room, there were no other vacancies. It was just for one night, tomorrow our paths would diverge. We would be strangers again, but not now. Not yet.

It was dark by the time we got back after having shared a sumptuous meal. The courtyard was enveloped by our silence. An uneasiness filled the non-illuminated atmosphere. Few words exchanged, each wandered on our own. I lost track of the boys and walked towards a portico, an in-wall arch. I sat on the steps. He was near, I could sense him. I felt his fingers caressing my hand. Caressing my arm, he drew me closer. Our bodies embraced — I could not resist.

    I wanted that night to last forever. Strangers no more.

7.
Travelling unreserved
Faith and fate

I was living in the Netherlands, with my classmate and soulmate for the last five years. The bubble we created on our first encounter was amazing. However, John's loyalty to his home-home girlfriend was stronger. During that first year, our encounters were a playful sensual flirting, but he stayed loyal. Transformed into a *Latina*, my pull on him grew stronger and eventually it was too hard for him to resist. Now we were together: John, my gentle spoken blond-haired, fair-skinned lover and I. His eyes, two grey-blue oceans speckled with seaweed greens.

Four years ago, John and I travelled together through the lush green South; through Kerala, Amma's motherland. Introducing John to my Indian heritage, I wondered whether his appreciation for me would increase. Would this plunge in an unknown culture broaden his worldview? Back then we skipped the most romantic place in India.

It was spring and we again were in India. This time around, travelling on the beaten track through brightly coloured and vibrant Rajasthan, bypassing the Taj seemed odd. The Taj Mahal; the biggest token of eternal love. Described as the jewel of Mughal art in India and one of the universally admired masterpieces of the world's heritage. I could not bypass it any longer. Was it going to be a way to express my love for him?

When we arrived at Nizzamudin railway station, we were greeted by the mullah's voice calling for Friday prayer from the Jama Masjid. Men clad in white *kurta pyjamas* and skull caps passed us on their way to the Mughal era mosque.

"John, we must go to the Jama Masjid. Mosques have this amazing serenity."

"Sure. We will, when we get back to Delhi."

My heart smiled, we oscillated on the same wavelength.

The train journey to Agra was an uneventful one in a 2nd class coach. We spent most of the journey engrossed in our travel guide and planning the itinerary for the coming days.

The next day, after having marvelled at the marble epitaph of love, we took a rickshaw to Agra train station. Thanks to John's Dutch punctuality, we had an hour to spare before the departure of our train. The train journey would take a mere hour.

My last minute change of heart however resulted in ending up with last minute unreserved tickets for the last leg of our journey. "No problem, that's how we travel, Kammy. I like it." John had responded when I told him we did not have a reservation on the train from Agra to 'Fatehpur Sikri'. "Seriously, are you going to travel unreserved?" Amma had questioned me. "Don't Kamala, not with John. Please just take a cab." She does not understand. A university student, I was not planning on spending our whole stash on a cab. I decided we were going unreserved for the last leg of the journey. As a child I often travelled by 2nd class sleeper to visit Ammumma and Muthachan. Like most middle and upper-middle class Indians, I never travelled in the unreserved compartment of an Indian train. Little did I realise what unreserved travelling meant.

As I walked past a food stall, I felt the heat of frying oil. "Aaah, yummy, freshly deep fried *samosas*."
    "Those look good." John responded.
    "Great, I'll buy a few for the train."

I removed one of the peas and potato-mash-filled *samosas* from the bag and held it so John could take a bite.

"Ouch, please hold it, it's really hot," I said, handing him the *samosa* and using a paper napkin to wipe off the oil from my fingers and take another *samosa* from the greased brown paper bag.

As we approached the platform, I saw the train already arrived. I walked to the booth located in the middle of the platform and bought a big bottle of water, for the *samosa* burnt my taste buds.

"We're lucky. I hadn't expected it this empty," I said with a broad grin, as we stepped into the train and looked into the compartment.

"Should we take these? They are closest to the exit."

"Let's take an upper berth, we'll have more space," I said to my Golden God, and added "take up as much space as possible," as I climbed up. Seated on the upper berth in the empty unreserved I was determined to hold my ground. There I was a twenty four year old fair-skinned girl with bunned-up hair, in hot sweaty Agra.

We settled in and stretched our legs. Between us we carried a mere 20 litre backpack. Unfortunate. I tried travelling light: clothes for a day or three, my snapshot camera, the Lonely Planet guide, two toothbrushes, soap, my paper diary, a pack of cards and a bag of crunchy *murruku* snacks. Over the past few years the realization that I lug along too much stuff had sunk in. 'Moksha, Nirvana' - get rid of worldly goods - was one of life's lessons I tried to put into practice. This revelation occurred two years ago when my luggage got lost in transit and I became aware that I could cope with less. Whatever I needed I could buy locally, and I often returned home having worn only half of the clothes in my suitcase.

An elderly man with a weathered grey toned face entered and sat on a corner of a bench that was still unoccupied. Another man, a young man with a walk indicating he suffered from polio, came and sat on the other end of the bench. He too took up as little space as possible. More people entered, mostly men, many with a greyish tone of skin, a frail posture or stoop in their walk. A lady entered in a *sari*. I noticed a few loose stitches on the blouse covering her upper body. We had one thing in common with the people in this compartment: the amount of luggage. They probably secretly observed us too. A thin middle aged man in a worn checked shirt came and sat on the bench below us. Another similar looking man was already seated. They were clean shaven. I nodded at the two men. A lady entered with a deformed face, outgrowths protruding in different angles from her face, neck and arms. I looked away. I felt sad, sad for her. Had she suffered badly from chickenpox or some other disease? My heart skipped a beat: could she be suffering from something worse, something contagious? Oh no, why had I suggested to travel unreserved? Why did I not heed my mother's advice? Why did I hold on to my socialist beliefs: everyone is equal? Humanist blood ran through every bone and nerve of my body, but I started understanding, to a slight extent, why some of my well-do-to friends felt such a disgust for 'these sorts of people'.

John checked his watch: 8:15am. The train would leave in another 15 minutes. By now, all the benches were over-occupied. I wondered how we would manage to hold on to our self-proclaimed territory for the journey. One sturdy looking man, dressed in a white shirt and brown trousers, was talking about us to the men seated on the benches below. He was telling them that 'the couple' should try and get a reserved ticket since they would not 'survive' in this compartment.

"*Haan, haan, haan* [39]," the men seemed to agree. At the next station it is going to become busy, he said in Hindi. I slapped my head

---

[39] Yes, yes, yes (Hindi)

with the palm of my hand. I understood what he said. I should have thought of this myself.

"John, we must get our tickets changed to reserved, if possible."

"Can we?"

"Yes, you have to find the TC, the Ticket Collector, and see whether they have space somewhere else in the train."

"They won't, why else do we have unreserved tickets?"

"Good point. Well, I don't know, but this man thinks it's possible and logical. Let's at least try?"

"Okay, so I go find the Ticket Collector?"

"Yes, you know what he looks like, right?"

While we were having this conversation, the whole coupe was in full attention looking at us and listening to our conversation. The sturdy man, who had mentioned the TC, now stood up and said he would take us to the TC, he said he wanted to help.

"John, you go while I stay here. If we are doomed to stay here, then I at least want some space for us to sit comfortably."

"No sir, thank you. *Nahi nahi, shukriya, khud kar sakta hai* [40]," I called after the sturdy man, as he exited the door following John onto the platform.

I poked my head out the window and saw both men. My gaze followed them till they reached the Ticket Collector. Hard to miss. The Ticket Collector wore a uniform and always carried a clipboard with a massive pile of dot matrix printed paper. I did not take my gaze off the men. Did I feel a certain responsibility towards John? After all, this was my motherland, I knew the culture. I knew what people meant when they shook their head sideways or slightly nodded or when they said yes and smiled or when… I turned my gaze from the three men to the inside of the compartment and understood I had made a BIG mistake. I had lost

---

[40] No, no, thank you, He can do it by himself (Hindi)

ground. I had left my stronghold, I had deserted our base. The upper berths, which a couple of minutes ago were ours, were now occupied by three men per berth. Six frail men who I knew would keep their ground. Their eyes ignored mine, clearly avoiding all contact. I saw John and the sturdy man walking back to our compartment.

"No space till Fatehpur Sikri, he said," John declared.

Agra to Fatehpur Sikri was merely a two hour journey, still I felt bad. "Shit. I'm really sorry. I haven't been the best commander in chief."

John looked up. "No worries, we will manage, Kammy," my ever-understanding better half said.

No words were exchanged, no eye contact was made. Sufficient space appeared, as if by magic. John and I sat on the bench opposite the clean shaven men. I felt John's sweaty legs touching mine. A thin air lining separated John and the elderly man. Personal space in India is almost non-existent, but here in this crowded area I noted that miraculously the accidental touching of bodies was painstakingly avoided.

The movement of air created by the train was refreshing.

"Where you from, sir?" the sturdy man asked John.

"Holland, the Netherlands."

"Ah Gullit, van Basten."

"Tulips, cheese."

"Windmills."

I was pleasantly surprised by their Dutch knowledge facts. Then the next question was raised, "Sir, how much tea costs in your country?" I hoped John would respond with a plausible estimate instead of mentioning the exact price.

On the top berth, I noted the men sleeping in shifts. Two men lying flat; one pair of toes in the vicinity of the nose of the other. I wondered whether they knew each other. The third man slumped up against the wall, feet resting on the ladder. Hardly anyone was chit-chatting, the noise of the train muffled all other sounds. I closed my eyes. The sound transformed into the erratic gushing sound of a waterfall, a soothing sound, a soothing movement of the train, the sun warmth on my face. I was dozing off. The horn of the train, in an alternating low and high frequency. A warning for cattle and people to keep distance, or a welcoming gesture to a passing train. I opened my eyes and looked out. Dwellings lined the train tracks and I noted the silhouette of a town in the distance. No pristine countryside or infinite space on this stretch, I reflected.

The screeching sound of the braking train. We nodded our goodbyes to our fellow travellers and left to explore the capital city of the Mughal empire of Fatehpur Sikri.

Having arrived at Fatehpur palace, we discovered our debit card was not accepted at the palace and there were no cash machines in the city. I peeked through the screens surrounding the palace grounds. I noted red sandstone architecture and open spaces. John took pictures with his SLR camera. Though the pictures would seem as if we had visited the grounds, the truth was we were banned from entering this magnificent cultural heritage. I became conscious of the fact that I had more in common with our fellow unreserved travellers than I realised. How does it feel to be barred from places, just because you can't afford it or are not wearing the right clothes or do not have the right appearance? I pondered on these questions for a while.

We wandered through a red sandstone arch and entered the buzzing market area. Pushcart vendors navigated their way through the maze of alleyways, promoting their merchandise in a monotonous way, naming the products in a singsong manner. An unbroken line of buildings, each containing jam-packed shops where stock and display intermingled. Goods to be sold hung from the sunshades and encroached onto the curb. For John such places were out of the ordinary, he discovered novelties in things that for me were mundane. He took a picture of a sweet-seller seated among his sugary delights and feasting flies. The sweet-*wala* gladly cooperated; he smoothed out his thick curled up moustache, the tips reaching his cheekbones. He sat upright, cross-legged and proudly posed for the lens.

Strolling through the city, we slowed our pace in front of uncountable steps. We were dwarfed. In the face of this 55 metres high stairway, we were diminished to insignificant souls wandering through this ancient city. The stairway led to a fabulous doorway, the 'Buland Darwaza'. Sandstone and white marble artisanal grandeur. Climbing up the stairs, the architecture gradually transitioned to human scale. On the other side of the elephant size door was the congregational mosque and tomb of the sufi saint Salim Chisti. It was a place of pilgrimage with intricately carved marble screens. I contemplated the exquisite skills and wondered about the ones we would not set eyes upon, the ones hidden in the barred off palace. After visiting the mosque, it was time to find a place for some refreshing tea.

"Pssst." I did not respond.

"Hello," I did not respond.

"Hello sir, ma'am," I stopped and turned around.

A barefooted young adult male was standing in a half opened gate.

"Where are you from? Please come in."

The usual exchange of Dutch knowledge facts followed. He was studying tourism, he told us. "Please come in, my sister wants to practice English," he said. Was this a scam or was it a unique and funny way of inviting a stranger in? I looked at John, he looked at ease. The gate swayed open and we entered the enclosed yard. Neighbouring children wanted to enter too, though our host hushed them away and closed the gate.

Next, we entered a sparsely furnished, but spacious living room. Steaming hot *chai* was served by his sister, Rusk biscuits were brought in by a primary school aged boy. Silence and smiles followed. What was the purpose of our visit?

"Sir, what is your good name?"

John replied "John," with a slightly puzzled look on his face.

"And yours?" I asked his sister, after all, she was the pretext of getting us in.

A shy smile lit up her face as she responded, "Komal."

"Then it was meant to be, for me to meet you," I said, adding "because my name is Kamala."

The mood changed. The ice was broken and we found our common ground. Komal told me she loved dancing and took 'Kathak' dancing classes twice a week. As the conversation progressed, I realised there was no ulterior motive for this invitation.

As the sun diminished in intensity, we were invited to the rooftop terrace. I noticed all terraces were interconnected, waist high parapets partitioning one from the other. I nodded to the next door neighbour hanging up the clothes, watched children flying their kites from neighbouring terraces. Looking down I spotted the single storey market sheds with corrugated iron roofs. I heard the mosque call out for prayer and Bollywood tunes float up from the shops below. The Buland Darwaza in the backdrop. Up here on this communal mazed terrace, a pleasant atmosphere prevailed, with no strings attached.

I got the sense of a tight knit community, a feeling of belonging. Here at this moment, descent and ancestry seemed irrelevant. We were all humans, sharing the afternoon sun and the bliss of small pleasures in life.

8.
Trust a stranger
Amador & others

"I don't know what's wrong. Maybe I should call the doctor when we get back." We disembarked and walked through the wobbly tunnel that led us to stable grounds.

"Is this the first time, Kamala?" Aleida asked.

"No, same thing two weeks ago, after the ferry crossing to Texel."

"It could be travel nausea," Aleida said.

"I don't think so. That would be weird. It is something else."

"Like what? Have you been feeling dizzy lately?"

There she was, my inquisitive doctor to be, testing her newly discovered diagnostic skills. Two weeks travelling with my soulmate, my secondary school best friend, Aleida. I was thrilled, and prepared. In posture we were similar, though I was 'blessed' with broad Indian hips and she with Dutch long legs. Stylish square red specs gave an extra sparkle to her radiance. Ours was a friendship at first sight. Cultural chameleons. Inquisitive about the world and a shared 'Dunglish' [41] humour. We did not keep many secrets from each other. Though, in the past, things were different. "I want to jump out of the window to fly, to feel free", as a fifteen year old, I confided in Aleida. She worried for me. She gave me a diary with a lock. "A pen friend to confide in when I'm not around," she called it. That is when I realised my intention did not coincide with her interpretation. As a teenager I gradually understood that some things are best left unexpressed. My reaction when I heard about her sister's miscarriage at the age of 16. Her anger at Pa for 'deserting' my mother and my brother in India. My pity for her and her siblings who took care of their mother after their father died. My desire to fly, to feel free, was yet another misinterpretation that created distance. Years later Aleida told me that she noted a difference in our interaction after her gift. She

---

[41] a mixture of Dutch and English

wished she could take it back, turn back time. She could not, no one can. Over time, our circle of friends expanded. Our expanding world, our experiences, and our understanding of caring for oneself and for others altered us. Our judgement matured and changed our perception of the world around us. In our twenties our rivers merged again.

At the Madrid airport we followed the sign *Alquilar coches* [42], to hire a rental car for the coming two weeks. That morning, I woke up with a twist in my stomach and a dull head. Trying to untangle it, trying to relax, I went to the loo twice and wondered whether I had drunk too much coffee. I knew I had not. I knew an irrational fear took hold of me each time I sat at the wheel of a car. I felt ashamed to share this with anyone, even with Lei. The fear that an accident could happen in the blink of a moment, irrespective of my own driving skills. Today, I wanted to face my fear, I wanted to overcome it.

"Kamala, do you still regularly measure your blood pressure?" Aleida's concerned voice cut short my inner struggle.

"No, not anymore."

"Why not? How's pressure at work?"

"Pff, not now Aleida. I've come to have fun," I said, grabbing her hand and shaking my head as I sang out "*Vamos a la playa* [43]*, oh oh ohoho.*"

"Well, ok Kamala, let's first find our hotel. After that you can take me wherever you want."

A "*Hola chicas,*" accompanied by a charming wink, came from the front desk chap as we approached. I smiled. It felt wonderful to be in Spain,

---

[42] Car rental (Spanish)
[43] Let's go to the beach (a Spanish song)

hearing sensual Spanish being spoken and picking up on unspoken messages conveyed through body language. But as soon as I saw the white Toyota, my stomach turned to stone.

"I'll drive first. Kamala, you'll be fine. You can drive the last hour." She knew.

The trip to Astorga was smooth sailing; no rush hour, no road tensions, no speed maniacs. As I manoeuvred the car in its resting spot, I was glad for spacious parking lots. Our temporary home for the coming two days was a slick white marble four star hotel, right across the regional tourist hotspot. The glorious Episcopal Palacio de Gaudí. Gaudí's work of art was amazing. I recalled Barcelona; I was mesmerized by his mind boggling and soothing zigzag patterns. I had been transfixed for hours. Fascinated. Today, as I stared at the grand structure across the road, I was curious to find out more on how Gaudí reconciled and incorporated his artistic hand with the strict Episcopal world view, which he needed to abide by for building this Palacio. Taking in the beautifully carved statues of apostles, I could not imagine a better location for our stay. I yearned for a front-facing room and hoped it would be granted to us; to two lovely charming young ladies.

"*Hola, señoritas que tal?* [44]" I turned around to face a man with a peacock feathered wide-brimmed hat and a 15 centimetre long salt and peppery beard. I had spotted him while turning onto the avenue leading up to our hotel. Instantly I had also noticed Aleida's guard go up. This eccentric man did look like a homeless old oddity.

"*Hola señor,*" I responded with a fleeting smile. I noticed the pleasant tone of his voice as he spoke to me in Spanish. Aleida got the bags from the trunk.

"What did he say?"

---

[44] Hello, how are you? (Spanish)

"He asked whether we wanted to go sightseeing with him, to the all-women's monastery," I responded.

"With him?"

"Yes." I winked and said, "Come, let's go in, there we'll be safe", trying to comfort my suspicious friend.

In our front facing hotel room, I peeked through the curtains and spotted the bird of paradise. His name was Amador and he was our guide to be. He seemed grounded at the same spot where we first set eyes on him. His eyes fixed on our hotel entrance. Is he waiting for us? I wondered.

"*Loco*. Crazy old man. Did you notice those stains on his frayed suit, Kamala?"

I let go of the curtain "No, I didn't."

"Yuck. How come you don't see that, Kamala." It was not posed as a question. No need for a response.

"You think he's homeless?" Aleida's muffled voice drifted from the bathroom.

"I don't know, but he doesn't seem to have anything better to do than to wait for us. Does he?" I responded.

Aleida emerged, her lips painted a vivid red.

"You look great," I said, "Come, *vamos a la playa.*"

"Shouldn't we wait a bit longer?" Aleida walked to the window. "I hope he moves on."

"Well, I don't plan to wait here all day just because you think someone is stalking us," I was determined not to give in to Aleida's paranoia.

"No, me neither, but…"

I locked my arm in hers and pulled her away from the window. "Let's go down."

We cautiously exited the front entrance. The bright afternoon Mediterranean sun lit up our faces as we set foot on the cobblestones. The tingling warmth was a pleasant change from cool Amsterdam spring. I did not spot Amador in the vicinity. What a shame.

"I am quite curious about the monastery," I said.

"What was so special?" Aleida had not grasped the information Amador conveyed in Spanish.

"I don't know, but let's go and find out and maybe we'll have a unique story to tell back home," I said trying to lure Aleida in.

"Well, okay. I guess there's no harm in taking free advice, without the 'madman' to accompany us," she said, bringing back the lightness into our trip.

We turned into an alley.

"You know, Aleida, in Texel, after I threw up, Paul acted like a moron."

"What do you mean?" Aleida replied, her eyes scrutinizing the alley.

"Well, he winked at me and said, can I congratulate you, Kamala." I sighed, "I mean come on, that was really stupid."

"Well, we have reached that age, Kamala."

"Oh, please Lei. That's not the only thing that matters, is it?"

As we left the alley and turned onto the main road, I scanned the street ahead. There he was, our bird of paradise, accompanying two middle-aged women. I poked Aleida and pointed across the road, "we're safe." From across the road Amador waved and gestured towards a house a few paces away, "*Las monjas* [45]" he shouted.

"*Gracias*," I mouthed back.

---

[45] the nuns (Spanish)

We walked towards the building he had indicated. The door was closed, and it did not resemble a church at all. "Definitely a madman."

"*Quieres entrar?* [46]" Our eccentric stranger miraculously appeared on my right hand side, enquiring whether we wanted to enter. He pushed the bell. We weren't given a choice: he wanted to be our guide. I did not want to admit it to Lei, but I was pleased he had left the ladies across the road and joined us. Was it the thrill and excitement of the unknown that got hold of me? Adventures are always around the corner, they befall those who are susceptible and open minded, I thought. The same holds for misfortunes, I know would be my grandmother's response. I do admit, I was also a tad apprehensive. I was dreading the moment that he might ask for a tip "whatever you think my services are worth, my dear." I hate such situations. No strings should be attached to human interaction. I felt sad and disheartened. At such moments I was confronted with the fact that 'No' was a word I had not learned to express easily.

"You do manage to attract strangers," Aleida whispered, eyebrows raised. Maybe Aleida's reservation was healthy, maybe it was good to question other people's intentions. Why couldn't I just say 'No'? Was I curious for new adventures or did I not want to sound rude? On such occasions I wished I had as well inherited some of Aleida's Dutch genes.

The door was opened by an elderly lady, dressed in black. My eyes needed time to adjust to the dark interior. Amador and the nun chatted merrily, as acquaintances do. I walked past the entrance door and stepped into the sanctuary. I marvelled at the comforting sound of the monotonous hymn, sung in an unseen place. Silence and hymns in such spiritual places create a sense of protection and belonging. A shelter

---

[46] Would you like to enter? (Spanish)

for all. I looked at the inner wall; reds, yellows and greens played a game of catch me if you can.

I realized we were being lured into Amador's world. Where and how would this trip end? Aleida came over to where I stood mesmerized. "Let's go out and leave him with the nun." I disagreed. "Amazingly soothing, isn't it? I wish I had been exposed to such spirituality earlier on in life."

Silence.

I turned to watch her face and saw the soothing effect that the reflections of glass-stained window had on her. I smiled. "I am curious to see what else he wants to show us," I said.

A tailor-made tour followed, past Roman remnants, an ancient bath house tucked away in the basement of a garage, and a special mature mulberry bush. The two of us would never have entered the posh looking marble façade hotel without Amador, the way we did. Amador was greeted with great amenity as he walked past the front desk and into the garden. Amador plucked mulberries for us and told us to cherish the moment. We were being given a royal treatment. We were eating mulberries from the same bush a princess had feasted upon years ago.

The tour continued and Amador entered a supermarket.

"Time to bid goodbye," Aleida said.

He re-emerged and motioned us to follow him in. Would he ask us to pay his weekly grocery bill? I did not care. He was a magnet and I was a nail. One can't change the laws of nature. I need to become a rubber nail, I thought, and grinned at my own inner joke. In the supermarket, people pleasantly greeted our Amador and the butcher offered richly aged *jamon curado*. Amazed, we looked through the glass floor at a Roman settlement below my feet. We were getting a unique insight into this city, seen through the eyes of a stranger, a local, a *loco*. I smiled and realized that any experience can become an adventure, if we want it to. A life lesson to cherish. I glanced at Aleida: did she realize this too?

The tailor-made tour ended at a bar for *pensionados*. A dozen elderly men and women, seated in the homely bar, were drinking local red wine for a mere 50 cents per glass. Amador offered us both a glass, we offered to pay.

"This is the real Spain, Lei." I stretched my back and flexed my muscles. In the aroma of dark red fruits, I took a sip.

"Where do we go next?"

"Let's just wander. Who knows what or who we'll bump into next." She had learned the lesson: trust a stranger and new doors are opened.

As we stood up to leave, Amador nodded and briefly took off his hat, "*Hasta luego senoritas.* [47]"

I beamed, "*Adios* stranger, *adios amigo.* [48]"

We waved Amador goodbye and strode off through a narrow alley. As we approached a plaza, I swayed to the swelling rhythm of a violin, guitar, and accordion. It was irresistible. Clicking my fingers and moving my torso, my face lit up. Finally, childishly merry we were, giggling away, oblivious of all. As we passed the players of the instruments, I smiled. Dark skinned men, their big well-fed bellies protruding, wearing the clothes of a wandering clan. In a few strides the trumpeter was at my side, he took my arm and swirled me around a couple of times, while the others continued producing up tempo beats. Before I realised what was happening, I felt another hand on my wrist. I was being spun in the other direction and then faced this dark eyed

---

[47] See you later, ladies (Spanish)
[48] Goodbye stranger, goodbye friend (Spanish)

black haired handsome Mediterranean man. Wow, he knew how to lead a lady in dance! Compelled, I moved to the beats as I obeyed my body's urges and needs. He drew me close and pushed me away, over and over again. The music felt as continuous as the ocean, rhythmic as waves breaking on the rocks. I tried not to look at him, at his eyes, for too long. It was hard to resist, intoxicating. I was excited. Breathless. We were strangers in this vibrant sensual Spanish city. Could this dance last forever? I wanted to cherish this intoxicating feeling.

A brief silence. As the musicians set in the next song, he eased the tension in his arm and our hands gently slipped out of our embrace. With a last swirl I exited the arena and he walked towards the other side. Strangers again.

  I wanted to look over my shoulder, to catch another glimpse of my Juan, my Don Quixote. What signal would that give off? The summer sun, a sweet-fruity *sangria* kick, what else awaited us?

  Aleida brought me back to reality. "Check your purse."

  I grabbed the zipper of my purse, "relax, Lei." Though, to be absolutely sure, I checked my valuables.

  "You do attract strangers," was her gloomy response.

  "Trust a stranger," I winked at her, "it is still something you have to learn."

  "Well, I am not yet sure that I want to."

  I slung my arm around her shoulder, "come, let's go and have some more fun."

  She grinned.

In a bar, sipping my fruity red wine and Aleida her fizzy drink, Aleida posed the unasked question, "So, you are sticking to your decision?"

  "Yes, definitely. I don't think it will make me happier."

  "Time will tell."

"Please Aleida, don't you too. Not everyone wants to have children, that's a fact. It's also a fact that people with children are unhappier compared to people without children." I paused, "I know you want them and that's fine with me." I paused again, "I do hope that we can still be friends."

"Kamala, you know that's unfair."

"Okay, then let's just leave this topic for a while. I am starving. I'll get a sangria jug; will you join in?"

"No, no sangria for me," she said.

"Really?"

"I am not sure, but I hope we'll be lucky soon." A meek smile crossed her face.

I blinked. "It's that serious is it?" I squeezed her forearm. Leaning over to give her a hug, I almost tumbled from my chair. We hugged and stayed in an embrace for a bit longer. "Super excited for you, Lei." I beamed, I was delighted for her and gave her another peck on the cheek.

I noted a profound look in her eyes.

"You know, I too have my doubts." She paused, "will I be a good mother?"

"You aren't your mother, Lei."

Her gaze shifted, she looked past me into the void. "Isn't it strange that we're grateful to our parents for our upbringing, but we also wish to be so unlike them?"

"Yes, I know. I want to pick some of their good traits, but definitely change what I dislike."

"I thought you weren't going to be a mom, Kamala."

"Well. I just mean, I understand."

"You know, the older I get the more I am like her. Will I be an overprotective mother, Kamala?"

"Time will tell, Lei." I gave her another hug.

9.
No entry
Joy of travelling

"Wait here," the uniformed man demanded as he took our passports and walked towards the office at the makeshift checkpoint on the road to Termez.

"I thought you're never supposed to hand over your passport," I whispered to John, when our taxi driver told us to give our passports to the guard.

"True Kammy, but we have no choice."

The guard motioned us to come in, we followed him into the steel container office. The guard was still holding our passports. He motioned us to sit in the soft-cushioned chairs with our backs to the wall. Our passports transferred hands. A young Uzbek man was holding our documents. He stood out. He was not wearing a uniform, but instead was stylishly dressed in a black shirt and khaki trousers, sporting classic style Aviator sunglasses. I noticed his symmetrical lips and a prominent lower jaw. An attractive man, I wondered whether he was the highest official on site. I sincerely hoped we were not being tricked and that this was not a hoax.

I felt tense but knew I should not show it. I hate checkpoints. We were being put in the spotlight, observed by invisible eyes. Those eyes crept up on me at US airports and at these less-used overland border crossings. Places where one was not sure of the rules and knew one was at the mercy of officials whose actions seemed erratic. Odd or unusual behaviour, in their view, could keep us stuck here for longer than we desired. I tried to act casual. Relax my shoulders, lean on one of the armrests, and stare at nothing.

The well dressed and fine featured man put my Belgian passport on the desk and was flipping through John's Dutch passport. I pondered whether having passports from two different countries made matters complicated. I wondered whether he would ask me to explain; why I, as a woman, was travelling with someone from a different country?

I am Belgian by birth and that is what my identity papers state, but am I truly Belgian? I have lived in India and the Netherlands. What defines who I am and where I am from? Neither my passport nor my nationality defines who I am. These are unimportant and do not disclose my uniqueness; my being. A few years ago, to make paperwork in the Netherlands easier, I tried to obtain Dutch citizenship. The Dutch, however, did not accept me. I spoke the language and was immersed in the culture, but I did not fulfil the required number of years of residence! I was not eligible for citizenship. I wondered: what does nationality mean in today's world? How does one answer the question "where are you from?" Here, stuck at this checkpoint, I had ample time to check my own thoughts on this matter.

"I'm a world citizen", is the unsatisfactory answer I often gave to this question: "Where are you from?" Yet I was not a world citizen, not having lived in many countries, only three. Maybe I would in the future. The joy of travelling definitely defined who I was. The joy of chance encounters and the discovery of common grounds and intriguing traditions. This joy of travelling starts long before my feet touch foreign soils. It starts with the anticipation of visiting a different country. Reading about the wonderful things to see, eat, and do. Reading about the local culture, and its history. Getting to know a new culture, its cuisine and marvelling at the natural beauty are reasons I travel. Connecting around the world, slowly becoming a world citizen.

Sunk into the soft cushions, nervously waiting for our passports to be stamped reminded me of another border crossing into another country.

Travelling from Peru to Bolivia, having another nationality made a difference. John and I changed buses at the border town of Desaguadero.

We could have easily walked across the border bridge, without any official stopping us, but to avoid hassles later on in our journey, we decided to get the stamps at the official checkpoint. The immigration official stamped my passport, hardly taking notice. However, on seeing John's passport, a doubt crept into his mind. He went over to the desk with the 'clear list'. Holland was not on the list, Belgium was. He called over to his colleagues asking them whether Dutch nationals need a visa. We kept quiet while the official sat thinking for a while.

I hesitated and said, "Quizas *las Pays Bais?* [49]", hinting at one of the other names for the Netherlands.

He looked at me and then stamped John's passport without looking at the clear list again. We were allowed to enter and were welcomed to the Bolivian pace of life.

I hoped the wait at this border-crossing in Termez would have the same outcome. I did not dare glance at my watch, I did not want to draw attention. Had we been waiting for an hour, half an hour? I did not know. Sweat started accumulating in my armpits. I readjusted my shirt. I kept telling myself: just wait silently and smile and it will all be over soon.

"Why are you travelling this road?" the slick-suited man asked.

"We're on our way to Tajikistan," John answered.

"This is not the way to Tajikistan — you are on your way to the AFGHAN border. Why!?"

It is exciting, that's why. Luckily John did not utter these thoughts.

"We were told this was the route. It is part of the ancient Silk Road," John replied.

---

[49] Maybe the 'lowlands' (Spanish)

"Wait here." The man walked towards the other guards and discussed while glancing over at us.

We were the only travellers in the office. We were on our way from one place in Uzbekistan to another place in Uzbekistan. This was not an actual border crossing. Why were we being scrutinised? I was aware that in some regions in Central Asia, special prior permission was required. I was not aware that we needed an invitation letter to enter Termez.

I knew that for John, the proximity to Afghanistan was the main reason for choosing this route. While browsing the internet, when he saw that only the river Amu Darya separated Termez from the Afghan border, he became excited. He dreamt of crossing the old white iron railway bridge that crosses the Amu Darya at Termez. It was called the Friendship Bridge. Yet I figured we would not be allowed anywhere near the bridge, even if we were allowed to pass the current checkpoint. For now, we were stuck in a container, no sight of the Friendship Bridge yet. "Tensions are rising in the area", our driver told us. Rumours were that next year the US military were leaving Afghanistan. I driver also told us more bearded Uzbeks had been sighted in the country. John told me he wondered whether this was the reason security was stepped up as we were nearing the Afghan border.

We could not do much now, just wait and see and let our minds wander.

------ The journey so far was wonderful. Travelling on the long forgotten Silk Road, stretching from Istanbul to Beijing, this was a dream. For years, I fantasized about this ancient road on which long caravans of Persians, Turks, and Chinese travelled to exchange goods. The caftan robed traders rested at splendidly carved 'Caravanserais'. I pictured them in my mind within the background splashes of blue hues of the gorgeous Islamic structures. It was as if I were watching an old blue and white movie. It was magical to relive this epoch by wandering through the ancient watering holes of Samarkand. The dazzling beauty of the Islamic architecture was something I was keen on admiring up close. Samarkand and Bukhara were some of the names I had heard as a child in stories my Amma narrated to me.

During this six week long trip, we travelled through a few of the stunning Stans — Turkmen, Uzbek and Tajik. Admiring intricate blue mosaic patterns covering the domes, minarets, and the majestic gates of the mosques and *madrassas* [50]. In Khiva, I discovered a *madrassa* to be a serene place. The empty square surrounded by walls on all sides with a lonesome tree in the middle. Within those walls were rooms and each room had an arch shaped entrance. All *madrassas* looked alike, only the hues of blue were different, as was the pattern on the walls. Each *madrassa* we visited exhibited the same calm ambience. Instantaneously I felt at ease. The burning afternoon sun made it impossible to rest in the square itself, but under the arches, seated on the pavement, I soaked up the atmosphere of bygone years in Khiva, Samarkand and Bukhara.

Less agreeable were the money-exchange practices in Uzbekistan. At the market in Khiva, John followed two Uzbek men with a big shopping bag stashed with currency: lots of it. I felt restless. I lost sight of the men and John. John had told me to wait and not follow him. He said he did not need my help because during currency exchange the international sign language and language of numbers would be spoken. This was a man's business, he said. He had been successful, but in the process I am sure I gained a few additional grey hairs. With our Uzbekistani Soms stashed

---

[50] Islamic schools

away in pockets and bags, we continued our journey through central Asia.

The languages spoken on this trip were tough to get a grasp on. Speaking Russian would have made travelling in these countries easier. For one, we would have understood what the guards here at the checkpoint were discussing. Though I doubted whether everyone here was fond of Russian and Russians. ------

We waited for more than an hour. I hoped we would be allowed through and that this wonderful trip would not come to an unfortunate end.

The highest official, the one clad in well-fitted clothes, finally walked over to his desk and picked up the telephone, dialled a number and talked to whoever was on the other side of the line. He flipped through the pages of our passports. I did not know whether this new change of events was in our favour or not. I could not understand one word from the telephone exchange. All we could do was kill time.

After what seemed like a long call, the man put down the receiver and walked over to us. "I have called the authorities. You do not have the right visa. You cannot pass."

"What?" I exclaimed "Why? What now?" I wanted to cry. What would happen to us? Were we doing something illegal? Tears welled up in my eyes. Our long cherished plan of reliving the Silk Road was being shattered. It was all coming to an abrupt end. I sunk further into the cushions, a black hole sucking me in.

Like a chameleon, the stern expression on the guard's face suddenly changed colour and loud laughter erupted.

"Hahaha, no I was kidding. You are set to go." The guard enjoyed his joke.

He handed us our passports. We were all smiles now and thanked the official and complimented him on his joke.

We exited the office and found our taxi driver near the building. I wanted to get out as soon as possible. One never knows whether such a tricky official will revoke his decision.

10.
The Russians are coming
for me

A two-lane asphalt road led to a pair of concrete square structures; one on each side of the road. One hole in the wall was used as a door and the other as a window. This was the immigration channel between Uzbekistan and Tajikistan. We had crossed over to Tajikistan.

A long river of trucks seemed to originate from the grey blob on our side of the crossing. Standing in the scorching sun on the Tajik side, I was greeted by a barren landscape, two apricot trees, two benches, and fellow border-crossers. A handful of cars were waiting. We waited, but we saw no car for us.

The back slapping, animated chatter of a bunch of middle-aged men, whom I figured were truck drivers, broke the natural silence. Some men were chewing and spitting out tobacco, others were smoking it. They seemed at ease with this pastime.

An elderly, friendly looking, wrinkled Tajik lady turned towards me. She leaned in and said something. I did not understand. I understood I could have passed as Uzbek. I wondered whether my Golden God would have passed as Russian. I smiled. The lady was clad in traditional clothes. Her peacock and pink coloured floral long *kameez* and matching flower-print headscarf made her stand out in this brown landscape. Two neatly trimmed grey-bearded men were standing in the shade of the apricot tree and turned to the lady. *Chet elik* [51] is the only word I could decipher; it meant foreigner. The Tajik lady, glad to have found new conversation partners, turned to face the men and continued chatting. In height and posture the men seemed similar, only the thickness of their beards differed. Black *taqiyahs* [52] decorated with white oval designs adorned their heads. At these moments I wished I spoke the local language or someone could act as a translator.

---

[51] foreigner (Tajik)
[52] prayer caps (Uzbeki)

A white van approached us, "Maybe that's our car."

The Tajik lady waved. The car stopped just short of us. The young driver walked to the lady, picked up her suitcase, and put it in the car. He opened the passenger door, she got in and they drove off. One more border-crosser abandoned our no man's patch. The two men, who were keeping the lady company, pulled up their trousers, flipped off their sandals, and made themselves comfortable on the wooden bench under the tree.

"John, when will our car come?" I asked.

"I don't know."

"How long must we wait?"

"I know as much as you do, Kamala."

We positioned our backpacks upright, leaning them against the bench and decided to follow the example of the men. It could be a long wait. Time was a relative concept along the Silk Road that we were travelling. Near the tree, three boys were playing a game with stones in the sand. Tossing pebbles one at a time, each tried to reach the drawn line as close as possible. After he flung his last stone, one of the boys stood up and walked towards us. "Where you from?" he asked.

"Holland," I replied with a sweet smile.

"Tulips, Euro, VanBasten."

He gestured to John for coins from our country. What a shame for coin collectors across the world, now with the introduction of the Euro, I thought. The boy pointed at my face and gestured with his hands the sign for "how much" and then, to make his intentions clear he said "100 dollars?" My facial expression changed, one raised eyebrow: I didn't understand what the boy meant. Surely he does not suggest buying me? No, of course not. Anyway if he were, then he would not be conversing with me directly and also he is too young for such deals. *Ttttchhh* why am I being so dumb and stereotyping, of course they do not do that here, buying brides in exchange of camels. What am I thinking? He gave me a big toothy grin and pointed at my mouth, to be more precise, at my braces.

"Ah," I smiled as I noted the boy's braces.

"A lot," I said and moved my arms far apart.

"How much?"

"Many hundreds," I said. Anticipating the next question, I brought my cupped hand to my mouth and added, "In our country a cup of tea is three dollars." Taking out our stack and showing it to him, I asked the boy, "Do you want to learn a card game?" A radiant beam on his face, he called over to his friends to join.

I turned to John, "When will our car come?"

"Kamala, I know as much as you do." John opened the zipper of his daypack and took out a plastic see-through folder. "Let me check." He looked through the papers, trying to find contact details of Tajik Adventures, our travel company. Was it a scam?

John turned to the elderly men and raised his hand to his ear, pretending to call on a phone and said "Can I borrow your PHONE?"

The eldest, the one with the stubbed beard, pointed towards the drivers and shouted out to them. One of the drivers walked over to us and raised his eyebrows in question. John repeated the phone gesture and said "phone, call Dushanbe, car." The man, clad in baggy pants and loose-fitted shirt, looked at the papers in John's hand and gave him his phone, gesturing it was okay for John to use it. John dialled the number of Tajik Adventures.

"Hello?"

"Hello, do you speak English?"

"Yes, Hello."

"Hi, we are at the border and waiting for a car to take."

"Sorry, who are you?"

"Oh, yes. Hi, I am John Jansen. We have booked a tour through your company and we were supposed to be picked up at the border. That is where we are now."

"I am sorry, we did not know you were coming."

"What?"

"I mean, the Uzbek driver was to call us when he dropped you at the border. We have not received a call."

"Now what?"

"Sorry, it is an hour drive for us..." There was a pause. "Sorry, are there any taxis there?"

"I don't know." John looked at me with a confused expression and mouthed the word taxi to me and raised his eyebrows in exasperation. I looked at the bunch of men.

"Taxi?" John asked the man standing in front of him, as he pulled the mobile away from his ear.

"*Da, da* [53], taxi," the man responded.

"I think this man has a taxi." John said, this time speaking into the phone.

"Does he look reliable?"

"Yes, I guess."

"And his car, does it look good enough?"

"I guess, I do not know which one is his, but they all look okay. Old but decent."

"Then you can go with him. Again, sorry for letting you wait. Can you hand the phone to the driver? I will give instructions."

"Okay."

John handed the phone to the driver. He put his ear to the phone and looked at us, "*da, da*". He smiled and gestured to us to follow.

---

[53] Yes, yes (Russian)

We heard a few more *das* exchanged, as the driver led us to his car. The white Toyota starlet with a crack in the front window was his.

The driver, with one hand on the steering wheel and the other holding a cigarette and resting on the window, manoeuvred the car, missing many of the holes. Driving like a maniac, sticking his head out at traffic blocked junctions, yelling. Yelling loud, but friendly.

"Are Belgian roads worse?" John joked, noticing the potholed condition of the road.

Minivans filled to the brim with melons drove past. Driving through villages, I saw stalls selling nuts and dried fruits. Men baking Indian-style *non* flatbreads. This all reminded me of Delhi, though the roads were much less congested here and the merchandise on the stalls was different. What was it that made me think of India? The hustle and bustle of a market place? The attires and the way people moved? I do not know. It was the feel of the place, the ambience, the *Maahol* [54] as they say in Hindi.

"Can we stop to buy some flatbreads?" I asked John and then uttered the universal word "stop" to the driver.

"We don't have any Somonis yet," my well-prepared better half responded.

"*Chalo, chalo,*" I automatically told the driver and gestured with my hands that we could move on. I really was in India.

After an hour's drive we reached Dushanbe, the capital city. The road system seemed orderly, the streets well-maintained and clean. No potholes here.

At the headquarters of Tajik Adventures, we met Omaid, our guide for the coming two weeks. Omaid was a lean man in his mid-thirties. His

---

[54] Ambience (Hindi)

English was fluent and easy to comprehend. It was pleasant to converse with Omaid on our personalised journey. This was the first time, on our adventures, that we were travelling with a predestined plan and the hotels and transportation were booked upfront. A way of making travelling in unknown foreign lands more accessible.

We exchanged Euros for Somoni currency in our communist-era high-rise hotel. The staff was friendly, but in our sparsely furnished room a depressing ambience seemed to envelop us. John switched on the AC and we tucked ourselves in for a comfortable night's sleep. Tomorrow we would go off the beaten track, hoping for a lighter mood.

Next day at lunchtime Omaid left us at a deserted place that gave the impression of a banquet hall for weddings.

After the meal: "Omaid, a local restaurant would have been okay. You know, right?" I tried explaining, for the zillionth time to our pleasant guide.

I had not yet figured out which mode of travelling I preferred: being chaperoned along by a guide, or much more on our own. Although travelling with a tour company had its advantages, I considered being taken to touristic eateries as one of the downsides.

After lunch we all hopped back into our off-road four-wheel drive and set off to our next destination: Iskanderkul.

I held my camera ready, ready to click. The road from Dushanbe to Khojand was considered one of the most scenic in Tajikistan, but first we had to pass the tunnel of death.

As we approached the Anzob tunnel, the driver turned off the ventilation in the car. It can't be that bad, can it? How am I supposed to hold my breath for the 5000 m drive through?

"Man, they are crazy, they must be Dutch," I exclaimed as I saw two fluorescent vests biking through the potholed dark tunnel in front of us. The driver passed them, making sure not to end up in a pothole himself. The driver was focussed on dodging the men at work and the numerous puddles. Omaid looked at us, grinning, he said,

"It was much worse. The Chinese are helping."

Gradually exhaust fumes filled the vehicle, replacing the fresh air. It had been worse? How bad can it get? I wondered, trying not to cough.

Then, I saw light at the end of the tunnel. Thank God. As soon as we exited the tunnel, John and I simultaneously drew down our windows. Fresh air. Mountain air pushed in and replaced the smoky air that had engulfed us.

"The Schiphol tunnel was closed for over a week, when the camera surveillance wasn't working well and lights were out," John said.

"Then they'd have to close this tunnel for years," I mocked.

"It wouldn't even be open to the public yet," John corrected.

As we emerged through the tunnel, I realised we were driving through the colourful Fann mountain range. Mountains on both sides, each with such distinct colours. We were familiar with green and white ones, like in the Alps and other tree-clad or snow-covered mountain ranges in Europe. Sitting in the back of the jeep I was stunned by the variety of shadings; each hill portrayed a different pattern. The slope to our left boasted dark red tinted jagged rocks protruding through the rusty-coloured soil. On our right, alternating layers of greys covered the earth with dark green shrubs spotted across. I could not stop clicking, even though I was being jerked from left to right as we made our way uphill. After an hour's drive the windy road brought us to a vista point. I was eager to disembark and take in the views of all the scenery we passed.

John gave me a hug and then slung his arm around my waist as we walked towards the ledge. I peeked over the edge and watched in silence. The white frothing aquamarine meandering river forcefully gushed through the valley.

We drove on and then there it was:

Majestic Iskanderkul.

Alexander the Great's lake with in the backdrop two brown dome-shaped mountains. The lake's colour changed from deep turquoise to shades of eerie green. The reflection of the dome-and face-shaped hills was mesmerizing. This stunningly located mountain camp 'Turbaza' was our home for the coming two days and was impossible to reach with public transportation.

I spent the day at the lakeside, leaving it only for a 30 minute walk to a nearby waterfall. The water was too cold for a swim. Being a photographaholic, I did not mind. The mountains and chameleonesque water kept me captivated. I sat on my bum on the cold sand and heard splashing and frolicking further down the bank. Did kiwis travel to this part of the world? I did not know. Most likely they are drunk Russians, I thought. The cold did not deter them from going in.

As evening set in, I met up with John and went for dinner in the canteen. As we entered, I realised that either many chalets were vacant or campers were dining elsewhere. The lakeside Turbaza consisted of 30 basic wooden chalets spread out over 10 acres. The chalets were set 20-30 meters apart, with a few green havens with shrubs, trees, and fireplaces.

Omaid had not informed us of his dinner plans and I didn't see him around. I was glad to be alone with John for a bit. I enjoyed travelling on our own — it gave us ample moments to interact with fellow travellers. In this region though, we required a guide.

In the sparsely furnished soviet-style canteen, the proprietor asked us whether we were staying for dinner. She gave us the menu. I got out my travel-guide and flipped to the pages with Tajik words and translations. Using the food section, I tried deciphering the food items.

"This is beef, shall we take that?" I asked John and pointed at number five on the list.

"*Njet* [55]," the proprietor replied.

I went back to my guide and pointed at number eight, another beef dish.

"*Njet*," was her response. I looked at the lady and asked "which one?" making a gesture by spreading out the fingers of both my hands trying to convey my question.

She pointed at number ten, the only dish available.

"*Da*," I smiled at the lady. After she left, John and I shared a hearty laugh.

"Just like in China, do you remember?" John said.

"Exactly."

During dinner we enjoyed the company of a French artist-cum-traveller. I envied his sketchbook. His way of travelling was extraordinary. Staying with locals, drawing and painting them in return. A wonderful barter system, no language was required. Would I be able to travel in such a manner in a country where I did not speak the language and did not know or understand the culture? I wondered. I was envious. I would love to travel the way he did. What did I have to offer? Only my smiles and understanding, and appreciation. Could I convey that without words?

---

[55] No (Russian)

After dinner, we went for a stroll, exploring the grounds. We stopped in a wooded patch on the campsite. We opted for the wooden bench instead of the picnic table. Soon I heard voices in conversation. The voices grew louder. I saw an elderly man with long thin wavy grey hair approaching us, walking towards the table. He was carrying a bottle of vodka. Behind him walked a slender, young woman with auburn tucked-up hair and a young big bald white male. There was no mistaking, the bald guy with pointy chin and narrow eyes was Russian. Both men were carrying boxes and bags. After placing all their goods on the table, the two men were on their knees at the fireplace.

"*Zdravstvuyte* [56]," the brunette called out to us, as she unpacked the bags.

Both John and I smiled and nodded back. I tried my Russian and responded, "Sradstuviet."

"Where are you from?"

"Netherlands. You?"

The leaping flames at the fireplace lit up the secluded patch.

"Russia and here. Come join us." Anastasia told us that they lived in Moscow. Her father was born and brought up in Tajikistan, but they moved to Russia and after years of absence now they were revisiting Tajikistan.

I could not resist the delicious pieces of grape-soaked mutton. An unknown taste. It was a delight to share food with locals. As I put the last piece of grapey meat in my mouth, I heard euphoric singing drifting through the woods. A little later I saw three men staggering towards our idyllic barbeque gathering.

The men spoke in Russian. They greeted us and joined us at the picnic spot, putting their bottle of liquor on the table. Bellowing out a

---

[56] Hello (Russian)

song, one of the men tried conveying the message of 'Sing with us'. The intruders were curious, they wanted to know who we were. Each had to sing a song, that was the game. Antaakshari, I muttered. Anastasia seemed apprehensive, she kept her distance and did not get too jolly. I could see her father and the bald man were used to such drinking games, they joined in.

"*Vader Jacob, vader Jacob, slaapt gij nog, slaapt gij nog* [57]..." John chose to recite a nursery rhyme when it was his turn.

The Russian intruder pointed at me, shaking his torso and circling his hips. "She can dance is what he is trying to say," Anastasia told me. I did not want to sing and dance in front of these drunken men. I felt ill at ease. The bald man seemed to be trying to divert the conversation. I detected a mood change in Anastasia and her friend.

"Come, come with me," Anastasia gestured for us to follow her. We did.

"We do not know what these men are going to do." Anastasia led us to her own chalet and bolted the door. She briskly went into all the rooms and closed the curtains.

"What is she doing?" I whispered to John "Why did we follow her? We could have gone to our own chalet instead."

Anastasia refrained from switching on any light and took us to a bedroom with two bunk beds. "You can sit on the beds. We can make it fun." Anastasia left the room and I heard the front door open. I heard voices.

"God, what's going on, John," I uttered in a hushed voice.

"Don't worry, it's ok, Kamala. They're nice people."

"You never know, John. This is weird."

---

[57] A nursery rhyme in Dutch, similar to 'frère Jacque'

Anastasia and her father joined us in the bedroom. Anastasia was carrying a pack of cards. She lit a candle, put it on the floor and sat next to it. I felt a weight lift off my shoulders. I joined Anastasia on the floor. John sat on one of the beds, he stooped forward.

"I can teach you a Russian card game," Anastasia started shuffling the cards and distributed them.

A sudden banging on the door.

Anastasia left the bedroom. We heard her unlock the front door. The bald guy came in. His speech was slurred, his eyes red. "I keep them at a distance, make sure they do not come looking for girls." He looked at me and left.

"With these drunk men you never know what they will do. We have to be careful." Anastasia told me. I wondered which men she meant.

"Vladimir is going to join the men and keep them occupied. They are getting REALLY drunk," she said. We continued the card game, though I did not grasp the game and randomly threw cards on the pile. My mind was preoccupied. I could not focus on a futile card game. An hour passed, nothing happened.

"Okay, now you can go to your chalet. Be quick, so that they do not see you." Anastasia directed us to leave.

Stumbling through the shortcut route, avoiding the street-lantern lit paths, we reached our chalet. My heart was pounding frantically in my chest. As soon as I entered the chalet, I shut the door and refrained from switching on any lights. The beam from a nearby lantern provided us with sufficient light to undress and get in bed.

I felt the muscles in my body still nervous from all the evening's adrenaline. My body was strained, I could not relax and did not fall asleep. That door was bothering me. It did not lock properly. One kick and it would unhinge. Where were the Russians? I wondered. I glanced over at John, he was sound asleep as soon as his head touched the pillow. I could get no shut-eye ....THE RUSSIANS WERE COMING....for me!

11.
Communist Cambridge
A cultural chameleon

Ente per Kamala aur main Belgium mein paida hui hun. Toen ik zeven jaar was ben ik naar India verhuisd, and now I live in Cambridge [58]. Oh, I am sorry, I did not realise you do not understand, nor speak these languages. I will continue my speech in English. I was brought up multilingual and multicultural and I must confess that this type of 'code-switching' is definitely one of the downsides of being multilingual. Of course there are also many advantages of being a multicultural person. Today, I would like to share with you my own thoughts on this subject.

Sitting at our one by one meter flimsy foldable dining-cum-study table, I was preparing for next week's Toastmasters speech competition. Being in multicultural Cambridge and surrounded by people from all over the world, some of whom were bringing up their children in a country outside of their own, made me reflect on being a cultural chameleon myself. Preparing for the ice-breaker speech was the first time I put such thoughts to paper and probably the first time I actively thought about this matter.

Staring out of the window of our new home in a seven-storied red-bricked condo close to vibrant Harvard Square, I saw none of its vibrancy. White was all I saw, a white haze. It was February and another blizzardy day. This morning John left for the office by bike, crazy Dutch guy. Roads were closed for motorised traffic. "The road is accessible," he claimed. I am glad he dressed warmly, lows of -20°C were expected for the Boston area. I wrapped my hands around the warm *chai* and looked

---

[58] My name is Kamala (Malayalam) and I was born in Belgium (Hindi). At the age of seven I moved to India (Flemish/Dutch), and now I live in Cambridge.

at the air-conditioner sticking out of the window. I fleece-plugged all the draft prone gaps, and wondered whether the covering would do the trick of keeping <u>out</u> the chill. Our one-bedroom apartment had been florally decorated by our landlady; not anymore. "'I will be the one stuck in this apartment when you are at work," was the complaint I conveyed to John. John disapproved of my spending on such trivial matters as goods for our apartment. But I needed to feel it was a home, especially as here I did not have a community of my own.

John was privileged to work at MIT for two years, so now we lived in Cambridge, Massachusetts. This was the epicentre of New England. I was on a self-proclaimed sabbatical; no 9 to 5 job to keep me occupied. Weeks before we crossed the Atlantic, I had a recurring nightmare. An apprehension of being stuck in a flat in suburbia USA, wilting away while John was at work. I hoped that living close to Harvard Square would partially solve the problem and provide ample distractions. These were my terms and conditions for our venture across the ocean.

From the onset of our stay in Cambridge, I made it a point to keep myself busy and to find a purpose. Tidying up the house was one of them, and surprisingly I found pleasure in such mundane household chores. It was of utmost importance to me that I would not be stuck in between the four walls of our condo. I made it a habit to leave our tiny apartment each day. I needed a purpose. Attending events and workshops where I could intermingle with people became one of them, shopping became the other.

At times shopping chores took up two hours a day; I walked all over town to different shops for different products and meticulously read the ingredients list before placing the product in my cart. I had understood to avoid added sugars, even in bacon!, and additives like

High Fructose Corn Syrup. Ordering an Organic-box every two weeks brought some peace to mind and challenged me to cook with unfamiliar vegetables like kale, turnips and sweet potatoes. Being able to eat *murruku* and *dosa* outside of India brought joy and briefly transported me back to India. The Indian store I loved, how I would miss that when we returned home to Europe. In the Netherlands friends and acquaintances assured me that the East Coast was similar to Europe, I would easily fit in. However, on my numerous grocery chores I never got accustomed to baggers, or courtesy clerks as they are also called. Chance encounters and chats with strangers, also during my shopping sprees, brought pleasure and gave me an insight into the community and country I now called home.

I looked at the clock: 10:30. In another half an hour the writing club get-together at the community centre would begin. I gazed out: the frequency of the snowflakes decreased yet their size increased. I took a last sip of *chai*, warming my throat as it eased its way down my body, and I set the mug aside. I took off my shawl and jersey, donned a fleece sweater and my down jacket and grabbed gloves, hat, and a muffler. I wrapped myself in as many layers as possible and set out by foot to the community centre on campus.

As I left the condo, all was white that met my eyes; no cars visible, not even the parked ones. To keep my mind occupied so as not to sense the brutal cold that hit my bare face, I invented a new game. Walking towards Harvard Square, I tried figuring out whether a car was buried under the snow heap I passed. Sometimes a protruding car mirror gave away the hiding spot. The tip of my nose was dripping. Cold and wet, I pulled up my woollen shawl. Walking through the red brick arch, I reached familiar ground: the campus. The red brick buildings and the spacious layout created a pleasant welcoming vibe. Though today the grounds were deserted.

As I approached the community centre, snowflakes reappeared on my red jacket and muffler. As they stuck on my eyelashes, I brushed them off. My cheeks were wet. I pulled tight the muffler and rang the bell.

No answer.

I saw a note pasted on the door. The notice read:
Closed, due to severe weather conditions

I should have checked the university website before leaving home. I cursed. The cold air was getting to my lungs, the muffler was not doing the trick, my breath wetted it. Searching for a dry patch, I readjusted it. I turned around to head back, but then stood still and gazed at the gothic structure in front of me. Despite the cold, my heart filled with enthusiasm and cheerful thoughts surfaced. The icicles hanging from the roof and pillars of the building were fairytale-like. Long thin spiky sheets of ice. Wonderful. As I walked down the steps, I saw various forms and structures formed on the branches of a tree. I marvelled at mother nature's creations; the tree's winter flowers. I looked around and realised I was in a white wonderland with no other soul. Winter can be magical.

I longed for chance encounters with strangers, but today all seemed deserted. Since my fingers started tingling and my throat was burning cold, I decided I needed to get something warm. I walked back to the red brick arch and then I was back on perpetual busy Mass Ave. Not today though, today no buses huffed on the snowy roads. There were, however, a few other crazy like-minded people out on the well swept pavements. Delighted to see OTTO's pizza open, I went in and was greeted by the warmth and mixed aromas of peppers, pepperoni, onions and mushrooms. Removing my gloves and rubbing my hands together, I tried to decide which one of the utterly thin-crusted pizza slices I would have for lunch. A sizzling hot pepperoni pizza was placed in the display case, an easy choice. I paid for Buy-One-Give-One. I appreciated that OTTO was part of this movement. With my purchase, I provided another slice for someone in need, of which there were plenty in Cambridge. I enjoyed the sensation of the well-baked crust crumbling in my mouth and the oil seeping through, creating a spicy lining on my palate. The ill-clad men, parked on the benches near Harvard Square, caught my attention on my first day in Cambridge. When I exited the subway, they asked for spare change. Today, I was glad to see none around. During my first few months in Cambridge I tried avoiding the homeless, I definitely did not chat with them. Over the past months though, I progressed; they had grown on me since. I started giving spare change and once in a while I bought an extra coffee or bun. Had I become more mature in dealing with the forsaken and dispossessed? Had I lost some of my 'Indian baggage'?

Back out in the bitter cold, the wind stirred up and I realised I needed to head inside and stay warm. I walked three doors down the road and entered the Harvard Coop bookstore. At first I was surprised to realise people used the bookstore as a library too, but by now I knew. I walked up the stairs to the top floor, bought a coffee and walked to one of the desks. I pulled out a chair at the far end from a thickly bearded elderly man. His weathered face seemed to conceal a bitter story, though it also possessed a pleasant and inviting vibe. I nodded and took out my laptop.

"Hi there, what do you do?" The initiative for the conversation was his.

"Hi," I smiled, "I am a writer," I told him.

"Perfect place to be," he said, "surrounded by books. Have you published?"

"No, not yet. The blizzard brought me in today. Maybe I will write a story about an elderly gentleman in a library," I said.

Bob understood this as his opening cue and he spilled out his whole heartfelt history. He told me he had taught at college, just like my Pa. Then his wife left him, she left him shattered and hooked on the bottle and other intoxicating substances. It was downhill from there.

"I have no siblings of my own. Her family was my family and suddenly it all fell apart. They all turned their backs on me."

"Do you have children?"

"Yes, but they live across the country, studying at colleges on the West Coast."

"Yes, I appreciate that is too far for them to visit often." I felt for him.

"Too far? They don't want to see me. Break-ups are evil, it brings out the worst in people. There is a foul game at play. Come Thanksgiving and I was all alone."

"Any colleagues?"

"Oh no, they are the worst. They are all a bunch of snakes. Academics thrive on another's misery or demise. Poisson." I saw the venom in his eyes, how to change the subject?

"I am not in academia," I spluttered.

"Good choice," he said. Had I provided the anti-dote?

"You seem well now, Bob," I said, trying to bring back the lightness in the conversation.

"God works in mysterious ways," he said. "One day, I was seated on a bench, and a young woman with a pleasant sunny face walked past. A halo of alcohol must have surrounded me. I must have smelt awful. She did not seem to mind or notice, she gave me a radiant smile and gave me a coffee."

I saw her radiance re-enlighten his face. I pictured the girl and smiled at Bob.

"You know, she reminded me of my own daughter."

"That's lovely," I responded.

"That was a turning point in my life," he replied. We continued chatting for a while and I offered him a coffee.

"Do your writing, child, don't mind me," he said and leaned back in the chair. I switched on my laptop.

I waited all day. I wanted to chat with John, to tell him all I witnessed and experienced during the day. When he came home in the evening, I was loquacious.

"You know this place keeps amazing me. It is so different from what I expected. Did you know OTTO joined 'B1G1' movement, great isn't it? and I found out that because I am a member of the library, I can get many other things for free too. Cambridge organizes so many free events and with the library card, I can attend many more and all for free. Surprising isn't it? And becoming a member of the library is gratis too. All free of charge. Amazing."

"You hadn't expected that in the US?" he asked.

"No, of course not. The most capitalist country in the world," I laughed. "It almost feels communist, except I guess for the huge number of homeless here."

"You've never visited a communist country, Kamala. You'll be surprised to see the poverty there."

"Well okay, point taken. You know, today I met this really lovely ex-professor. Currently he is a homeless man. It was interesting to talk to him and it made me realise that homelessness can happen to anyone, especially here in the US."

"You mean because there's no social security system in place?"

"Yes, and because bad fortune can befall any of us."

"Yeah, well you know it is a combination of bad fortune and bad character."

"Come on, you know that is not true, not always at least. Social cohesion is important. Like in India. People help each other."

"Kamala, are you serious, like in India? You're being naive now."

"Well, okay, but social cohesion is important too, and I haven't yet figured out how strong the social cohesion in Cambridge is. In the US, I know it is weak."

"You don't know, Kammy."

"True, point taken. There must be a pretty good reason why Cambridge is fondly nicknamed as the people's republic of Cambridge."

"For American standards Cambridge is a very liberal city."

Wanting to change the subject, I asked, "Are you hungry? It must have been tough biking today."

"Yes, starving. Whatever you made, smells really good."

With a grin I responded, "One of Ammumma's specials. I am amazed I am able to cook on this weird electric stove."

"Turning out to be a kitchen princess." He winked. "Thinking of a career shift?"

I laughed and brought out the food.

After dinner, John pulled out his laptop; he needed to work. I opened my notepad. I wanted to remember and to cherish our time spent in this amazing place. I laid the foundation for my own community in this foreign land. I became part of the MIT Spouses & Partners group. In Belgium and the Netherlands, I was unique, here I was one of many cultural chameleons. Here I belonged, among like-minded and similar people. Couples from two different nations and young adults who were born and brought up in different countries, living in a land that is not their parents' country of birth nor their motherland. We were all in the same boat — the same world. We all wanted to help each other row the boat to a safe and enjoyable haven. Social cohesion. This MIT Spouses & Partners group was where I started building my community in communist Cambridge. I started writing in my diary. Recalling; Jacky from China, Tabuleh from Iran, Maria from Mexico, Jessica from the UK and Sandy from the US. We were all in the same boat, the boat of uncertainty and fear of loneliness. Together we discovered the stages of honeymoon and 'disintegration' during the process of cultural adjustment to a place we now called home.

The following week on Thursday, it was time for my ice-breakers speech. The sun was shining as I embarked on yet another day of explorations and enjoyable encounters. No blizzard and no snow today. I strolled down our road to the perpetually busy Mass Ave. I boarded the subway and disembarked at the MIT T-stop.

"Hi Kamala!" Sandy called out.

Glad to meet a friend. Together we walked to the Physics department, ready for the Toastmasters session.

Claire opened the meeting by welcoming all members and newcomers, before saying "Okay Kamala, whenever you are ready," and then she waved me on to the front of the room.

"*Ente per Kamala aur main Belgium mein paida hui hun. Toen ik zeven jaar was ben ik naar India verhuisd* and now I live in Cambridge. Oh, I am sorry, I did not realise you do not understand nor speak these languages. I will continue my speech in English. I have been brought up multilingual and multicultural and I must confess that this type of 'code-switching' is definitely one of the downsides of being multilingual. Yet I find many advantages of being a multicultural person. One advantage is that it is easy to learn new languages and it is easy to understand people, regardless of whether we speak the same language. A multilingual learns to understand through context, gestures, and emotions. Today I would like to talk to you about the advantages and consequences of being multilingual and multicultural and share my own experiences with you.

For every person, whether they are mono-cultural or multicultural, it is impossible to fully understand oneself. To know what we really want. Figuring this out, is part of the journey of life. Being multicultural makes this process even harder. Every event in our life changes the course of our life and the way we perceive the world around us. Everything that you experience and everything that you do has major consequences for what is to come. You are the only constant factor in it.

Preparing for this ice-breakers speech, I read on the internet that multi's or cultural chameleons as we are also known, share an understanding that there is more than just one way to look at a situation. I personally believe an increased exposure to a variety of perceptions and lifestyles creates a higher sensitivity to other cultures and ways of life. I enjoy and seek to learn about the complexities and habits of people from other cultures. True, I do not only see the positive aspects in different cultures, I also criticize certain aspects but I try not to focus on those. ==I must admit, I am still in the process of trying to unravel the complexity of the American system; my special interest is its social cohesion and cultural bonds.== I could continue to talk for hours on this topic, but I have run out of time. I would like to wrap up by saying: Variety is the spice of life.
Thank you."

I looked around the room, and saw smiles on many faces and a few appreciating nods. I beamed, as I realised my story resonated with my audience. I was expanding my community in communist Cambridge.

12.
Why do I always lose my husband?
Trust

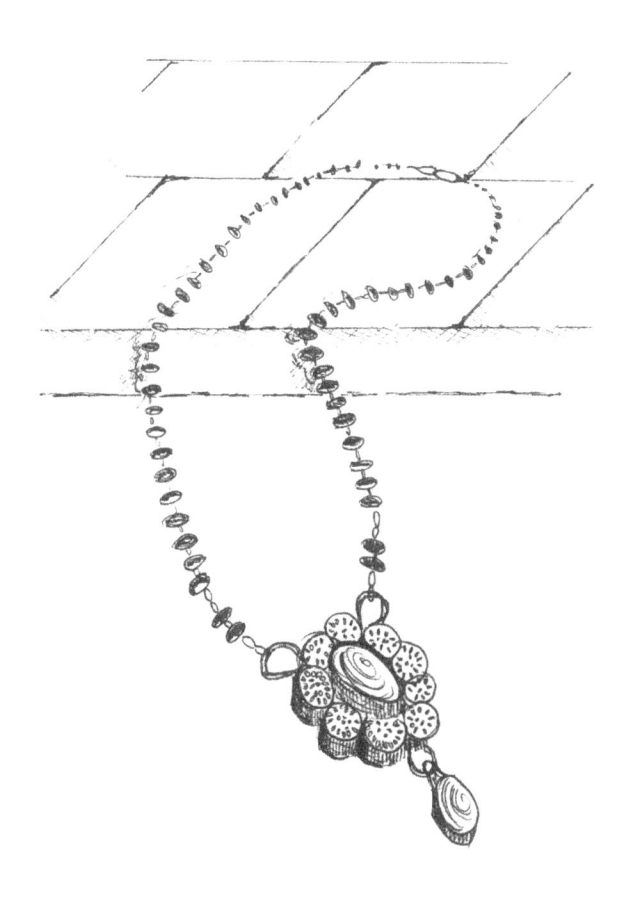

We were heading to Mount Desert Island, a getaway from workaholic Cambridge. The national park is located North along the East Coast in Maine. I had not done enough planning for this trip, though, and John spent too much time on his scientific research.

"We'll stop in Cambridge. Better safe than sorry," John replied when I told him I was sure of a cash machine en route. John was driving and our first stop was on home ground; Harvard Square. John decided to draw cash and I popped into a CVS pharmacy located in the Square.

"I'll meet you outside the…." John called out as I passed through the sliding doors. I felt a tad stressed as I marched through the aisles. I wanted to ensure that both of us were out at the same time. I sinned. Chocolates, crisps, nuts and cookies, I probably bought more than we would be needing for a week. I had been quick at it, though, I knew John had no reason to complain.

"Why do I always lose my husband?" I am sure I said it out loud as I frantically spun around 360 degrees. Where did he go? I don't understand. Where is he? I peeked into the Santander bank, maybe he was at the front desk. He wasn't. As I stood there, scrutinizing every person out on the streets — on my side of the pavement, on the opposite side, crossing the road, waiting at the T-stop — I was transported back to Delhi many years ago. The exact feeling took hold of me today.

>   Someone must have abducted him.

What an absurd idea. Who would abduct a 34 year old man in broad daylight in hectic Harvard Square? The previous time I had more reason to worry.

------ It was John's second visit to my motherland and I lost him. He had been unaware of the threat, I more so. I felt a certain responsibility for him. Love too.

Amma lived in a resettlement colony in Delhi. In the past this area was a slum with temporary dwellings, now most houses were built of brick. Some alleys were still narrow, just half a meter wide, with open gutters on both sides. Amma was not a typical slum dweller, but after I moved to Belgium for schooling, she decided to live and work with the less privileged of Indian society. We had visited Amma on our previous trip to India. John was familiar with the neighbourhood, but it was not the type of society he was brought up in.

On our second day that March in Delhi, Amma, John and I spent an afternoon at a local artisanal shopping complex for handmade goods. This was an oasis of quiet compared to the bustle beyond the walls of the red-brick enclosed compound. We ate authentic Indian *samosas* and tangy-puffed-rice *bhel puris* and listened to both professional and amateur musicians. After having spent some fun-filled hours, we decided to head home. We flagged a sturdy cycle rickshaw controlled by a seemingly fit driver. We left the shopping complex by 6:30 in the evening, which meant it was dusk by the time we arrived at the outskirts of the resettlement colony. The weekly Wednesday 'Buud Bazaar' [59] market was ongoing. At the Buud Bazaar people shopped for clothes, pots, books, fruits, vegetables and other day-to-day necessities. For most people in this area, this was the most important activity of the week. If you have ever been to India, you know how chaotic an open-air market can be.

---

[59] Wednesday market (Hindi)

"It will take ages for our rickshaw-*wala* to manoeuvre through this crowd. We will be much faster walking home. Are you okay with that?" Amma told us as she asked the rickshaw-*wala* to stop.

I acknowledged it would require a miracle to get through by rickshaw; like the sea parting for Moses or the river Jamuna parting to let baby Krishna be carried to safety from the tyrant king determined to kill him. Well, this was a sea of people, but I did not believe in miracles. We disembarked from our chariot and bid our rickshaw-*wala* farewell with the offering of some rupees.

Dusk in India is short and by now darkness had fallen in earnest. The merchandise on display was lit by gas lights, street lamps and torches. In a single file we set off for home: Amma, then me, followed by John. Being an enthusiastic photographer, John was keen on taking as many pictures as possible in this magical setting. Amma, oblivious of this magical touch, marched on ahead. She often shopped at this Buud Bazaar. I was the tour leader. Turning around to see John taking a picture, I shouted out to Amma or hurried towards her, asking her to stop for a moment. When John finished taking a picture, we could move on. This worked fine till we got to the butchers.

The butchers wore few clothes, men chopping away with sturdy knives. The pitch black backdrop behind their stall and the faint lighting was superb for creating an intriguing ambience. It was also a challenge of skills. I realised John would require additional time to adjust his aperture to the dim lighting and would have to stay fixed in one spot for a while. Not twitching and not being bumped into. That seemed an impossible feat in Buud Bazaar.

I watched John taking pictures. Amma, absorbed in her own bubble, was too far-off for me to shout and be heard in the Buud Bazaar noise of buying and selling. I wriggled my way through the crowd. When I reached Amma, I turned around and saw John was still clicking away. We turned to look at combs and other hair accessories on display on the stall behind us. When I turned back to check on John, he was gone.

"Amma, can you see him? I can't. Where is he? How come I can't see him? He was here just a few seconds ago!" I panicked.

"That is strange. I do not see him either. You would imagine it would be quite easy to spot a blond Dutch head in a sea of black hair."

"Amma, what do we do now? He doesn't have a cell phone and I am not sure he has your home number nor your address. Oh my god. Amma, what to do now?"

"Let us just wait here. He cannot have gone far, he will come back."

"Amma, maybe he has gone ahead and tried to find your home on his own." Panic took hold of me. What do I do if he goes missing? Should I go to the Indian police, will they help me? Will he have gone and asked a police officer? How well do I know John? What would he have done? Yes, he must have made his way home I was sure, but had he taken the right route?

"Amma, John asked me whether this road goes to your house. I said it does. It does, right?"

"*Haan.* Yes, it does." Amma pulled out her cell phone, and called home. The maid answered. "Has my *damaad* [60] come home yet?" Amma asked. It seemed he had not, the maid was home alone. We explained the situation and hurried back home, then I stopped in my tracks.

"Amma, ask the butchers. I am sure they know more." I whispered, staying close to her. The lantern lights made these men, with knives and dressed only in shorts and white tank-top undershirts, look evil. The dark park at the back of their stall made the whole scene even more disturbing. I realized what had happened. These butchers, who

---

[60] son-in-law (Hindi)

were now avoiding my gaze, had grabbed the camera from John's hand and thrust him in the bushes behind their stall. He must be wounded.

"Please Amma, ask them." She did not. We waited for a while; no husband. We decided to go home and deliberate about what further actions to take. At the next intersection Amma turned right.

"Amma, you said this road leads home. I didn't realize we had to take a right. Oh no, he will never find his way back." I increased my pace and continued on the road straight ahead. It did NOT lead to Amma's house, but it was the road John may have taken, if he wasn't lying wounded in the bushes.

At the end of the road, where it met the main road, I stopped. I scanned the curb. No John. I felt helpless. I felt sweat trickle down the back of my neck and some on my abdomen too. No John. I spun around, rushed home and ran up the stairs to Amma's first floor apartment. By now I was sweating all over.

There he was. He was seated on Amma's couch and Saroj was offering him a glass of ice cold lemon water. I had never been happier in my life than at that moment.

"I'm so glad you're here." I flung myself into his arms and gave him a long sweaty hug.

Saroj left us and went to the kitchen. The strong smell of black tea. In a reflex my body relaxed. *Chai* works miracles. A hint of chilli and deep fried onions entered the room. My stomach grumbled, yes I needed to replenish my energy spent during the search and rescue mission.

"I walked to the end of the road. That wasn't your home so I retraced my steps," he narrated how he navigated back to Amma's house.

When he reached home, he was surprised that we weren't there. If only he knew.

Crispy onion *pakoras* accompanied the *chai*, on the platter carried in by Saroj. I held the warm cup in my hands and blew at the *malai*, to ensure no skin was formed. It was one of the few things I detested with my whole gut, boiled milk. While blowing at the hot liquid I sipped the tea.

"Man, it's crazy; you manage to stay relaxed under all this stress." I said, adding "From now on, please stay at my side."

"Kamala," Amma called out. I grabbed a *pakora* and went to help Amma. Peace and order were restored. ------

Today, as I stood waiting for John I tried to text and call him. I knew he was fine, no abductions or injuries had taken place. It was not nerve-racking this time, but it was irritating nevertheless. I wanted to know where he was, we were on vacation together. Why didn't he answer my call?

I fidgeted with the black beads on my wedding necklace. This gold chain was given to me by Ammumma as a sign of belonging. I felt an arm on my shoulder and I turned around to look straight into John's eyes. We were linked for life.

I made a wish and a resolution: Never to lose my husband again.

13.
The next adventure?
A journey into motherhood

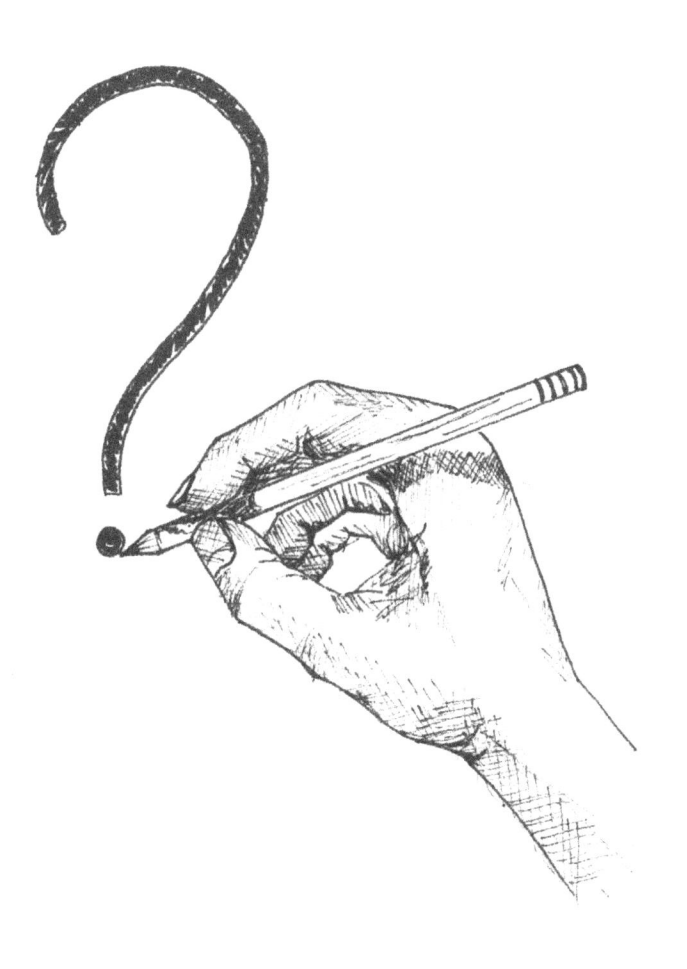

I rush down, Iqsha still asleep in the co-sleeper. I gobble down granola with yoghurt as quickly as possible. I wonder whether she will let me shower this morning. Thankfully today, she will spend the morning at daycare.

Walking back home, after dropping off Iqsha, I notice the intense light blue of the morning sky. This blue reminds me of Ammumma's lettered envelopes. I keep them stacked away in our attic; boxes full of letters and postcards. Gone are my days of puttering about in the attic and taking journeys down memory lane. A faint smile crosses my lips. Will I have an hour to spare today?

When I reach home I notice my mum-to be-diary lying lost in a corner. I flip through its pages. I no longer have a bump. I have a baby instead and a bigger belly to show for that achievement. Yes, I am a mum now. I myself never expected to be a mother. Or maybe that is not entirely true. I remember, as a six year old being questioned by Pa,

"Kamala, what do you want to be when you grow up?"

"Mother," was my immediate response.

It was not what Pa intended for me, so he tried again "And after that, Kamala?"

A pause. "Grandmother," was my most obvious response.

As I scrutinise the ultrasound image on one of the pages, I wonder: does the face bear any resemblance to the baby I have now? I read the expectations I jotted down in the diary. How naïve I was! It is THE universal job, our common denominator, but that does not make it any easier. The humongous responsibility one has, and the constant bombardment of choices and dilemmas. It is something I was not prepared for. Being a parent is something one can't prepare for.

It's become hard to recall those first few weeks of Iqsha as a newborn. Exhaustion I remember. I felt useful, but not the way I had expected. I was a feeding robot. Spending all morning upstairs. Life was so different when I was caring for Iqsha. I had to reassure myself each day and keep going on the treadmill of parent life. I put my own requirements and needs last, I put them on the back burner. No one made me do this, it just happened, mother nature worked her way. Now, seven and a half months later, I often still struggle to find my balance on this precarious seesaw of motherhood.

"I dread the days I am all alone with Iqsha", a week ago I confided in Christine, my middle-aged neighbour and a mum herself. "We mums all go through this phase, my dear," she said and then reassuringly put her arm on my shoulder. Then she gently stroked Iqsha's head and added "You know we are here to support you, you know that, right? Mothers for mothers, always." ==I was overwhelmed by this sudden soul-to-soul connection with my neighbour whom I had known for years.== She reassured me to call her anytime I needed assistance or me-time. I still have not taken her up on her offer. I wonder why? Does it feel like I am failing as a mother, if I ask for help? I find it tough to admit I can't cope. All alone with Iqsha for days on end, I know I will surely have a nervous breakdown. I know my village needs to expand. I have to rebuild my community, as I did in America. I am a mother now. I should accept her offer, I should, I will. Maybe this week? John will be abroad for a conference in Stockholm.

A message pops up on my screen in the baby group. I see a picture of Lot sitting upright without support. I smile. How different I felt about messages in this group during the first months. These other mothers, with babies the same age, shared how much in love they were with their baby, their bundle of joy, the love of their life. I remember how I read the messages, then lost the thread and went back to staring in infinity, focussing on the job at hand: keeping my baby alive. I scroll up to find my favourite message from six months ago.

1 December 2019

Eva
Lot sleeping nicely now. She cried, but didn't feed her stroked her head, put my hand on her chest
She fell asleep , what an angle <3 !!
14:22

Yes, same here 2 weeks ago, should have shared 14:27
unfortunately didn't work last night ☺ 14:28
Had to feed 2x!! ☺ 14:28

Sara

it's a phase it's a phase it's a phase,it's a phase it's a phase it's a phase it's a phase it's a phase it's a phase it's a **monster** it's a phase it's a phase it's a phase, it's a phase it's a phase it's a phase it's a phase it's a phase it's a phase
14:33

Sylvia
An eye-opener! 14:33

Eva
Hah, a monster! Yes indeed! 14:34

Angel last week, monster yesterday
Do hope it is a PHASE! 14:35

Sylvia
Yes, past results are no guarantee for the future ;-)
14:36

Sara
Yes, no manuals for these little monsters. 14:36

Judith
We mom's inventing the wheel all over again! 14:37

Eva
Yes, wish I'd pooped out a manual too 14:38

Sara
Haha, yeah!
I wouldn't have given a shit at that moment
LOL 15:00

In the first few weeks after Iqsha was born I did not know what I felt. Warmth? Yes. A bond? Yes. Love? I did not know. I had opened up to the group, sharing my feeling of helplessness, a sense of failing to meet her needs, failing to feel unconditional love. Tears running down my face, my vision blurry and unable to see the words I was typing. They responded, some sharing the same feelings, some opening up and sharing their own despair. We bonded stronger. We shed our masks and formed our own little village. We acknowledged: our eye's apples could sometimes be little monsters too.

Messages keep on appearing in the app. I will read them later. Today I want to remember. I open the conversation with Lei. This is my diary now. I easily forget. The initial dispiriting postpartum period cast a spell on the pink lining of motherhood. What happened? Now, a few months down the drain, it is hard to recall those initial feelings. I remember how I wondered whether I suffered from postpartum depression. I read about it; it was common in young mothers. I reassured myself I was not depressed, then later I speculated again, maybe I was suffering, just slightly? This sudden onset of constant uncertainty had been exhausting; it still was exhausting.

I look at my watch: 10:00. I need to vacuum the carpet.

While vacuuming I recall my recent unpleasant conversation with John. He and I seemed to drift apart. Had we started living on two different planets? This is what I was afraid of, I read about it in the Parents Today monthly. People stop communicating with each other. Stress and chores at the office pile up, as stress at home soars rocket high. Spouses stop communicating and start living in parallel universes. Is that what is happening in my life too? It happens in so many families, why will it not happen in mine? Am I exaggerating? Are hormones playing games with me? I sigh. Go with the flow and take it easy, I tell myself.

I go to the kitchen and make myself coffee. The sound of my phone ringing. It is Aleida. Shall I pick up?

"Hi Kamala, glad you picked up. Thank you. How are you coping?"

"Actually, remarkably well, I must say. Though I still need to eat and pick up Iqsha before one."

"No worries, we'll keep it short. Just so glad to hear your voice."

"Yes, me too." I smile. "You know, today I hope to spend some time in the attic in my archive." She knows. "Do you still have any of the letters I sent you?"

"Yes, definitely, though I don't know where."

"We should piece them together," I say.

"Yes, when we have time." We share a laugh.

"I need to get some fresh air. I need a breather, you know. I just don't manage to get everything organised in time. The same story, every day," I complain. "How do others manage?"

"It's okay Kamala," Aleida says.

"Well, it's past 11, I just made my first cup of coffee and my house is a total mess."

"Those days happen, Kamala. Don't worry about the little things," Aleida reassures me.

"In my case, it's every day, Lei. I am sure that's not okay," my voice breaks. I close my eyes and take a deep breath.

"Hey, but we finally managed to call today. That's an achievement."

"Yes, I guess. Well, Iqsha is at daycare, that's why." Then I add, "Sometimes I really don't know how I will get through a day, you know. I don't understand what I do wrong. How do others do this? How do you?"

"Hey, Kamala, relax. Take it easy and just believe that germs are good for a child's immune system." She continues trying to convey the lightness of being. I stare at the trees swaying gently across the road and take another deep breath to get a grip on myself. I exhale.

"Do you know why I called you?" she asks, changing the topic.

"To hear my voice," I respond blatantly.

"That too, but I was reading through our messages, and I needed to speak to you," she says. "I realised we've had so many revelations the last few months."

"Yes, I know, now that we are mothers." I finish her sentence, knowing exactly which messages she read.

"Absolutely. Parenting is tough." I hear Aleida exhale.

"I know and mine hasn't even turned one yet," I confess. Then I add, "I can't comprehend how your mum managed on her own and that too with three kids."

"Yes, I have so much more respect for her now. It's unbelievable."

"Yes, we start forgiving them for some of the mistakes they made." I smile.

"Parents are normal human beings, and yes none of us is perfect. Don't forget that, Kamala." I hear a kiss being transmitted through the phone.

I shower. Then I go up the steps to the attic, down memory lane. There are my memories all sorted in boxes and marked; Vacations, Pregnancy, Letters. As I rummage through the Letters box my eye meets postcards and scribbles from secondary school friends on letterheads with teddy bears and floral designs, covered with hand drawn hearts. Postcards of beaches and French rolling landscapes. Each one with untold tales to tell. Looking through the box I wish I had the other half of these letters, the ones I sent out. Do others hang on to letters for memory's sake or is this habit peculiar to me? Have my peers 'Marie Kondoed' away all their memories, I wonder. To me, writing is remembering. Remembering is cherishing. My eye falls on another see-through box; scraps of papers, plane tickets, a miniature Tadjik flag, a camel-hair camel figurine. Travels and adventures. I wonder: will this box be filled with additional memories? I slide forward the box and delve in, pulling out all the knickknacks and piling them on separate heaps. Each mound represents a different trip. I love this process; I call it cleaning up. Going through all these keepsakes and recalling memories. A chaos is created and it takes a while before order is restored. I know John disapproves of my methodology, but he is not home now. These are crucial parts of my life, stuck up in boxes.

I look at my watch: 12:45. I need to head out, I need to pick up Iqsha. Letting the piles be piles I rush downstairs, grab two slices of raisin-bread and stuff them in my mouth. I grab the keys from the dining table, the baby sling from the hallway, and step out into the warm afternoon. Out in the sun, my head spins back to the conversation. It is such a life changing moment: becoming a mother. Suddenly someone else determines your whole life and what you can do with it. Suddenly you stop being an individual, you become a parent and your life is dictated. But parents are individuals, too. I believe people don't flourish when they aren't able to live their life to the full and are caged and pulled down by societal restrictions and dogmas. When people don't flourish, they aren't happy. When people aren't content or happy with themselves, they can't bring joy to others either. Being pleased with oneself is the key. The prospect of not being in control of my own happiness, was something that for a long time kept me from taking this plunge into motherhood. That was something I did not want to sign up for. Who was to tell whether my child, if I had a child, would turn out to be a merciless dictator, an empathy lacking psychopath, a …. or the love of my life. I had seen the motherly bond sprout between Aleida and her firstborn. It was a sensation which I found hard to describe, but sensed intensely when I first set eyes on mama Aleida with her baby Tim. They were in their own little world — a bubble which was theirs alone. Later on, when other dear friends stepped over the threshold into motherhood, I experienced the same powerful sensation.

I pause my string of thoughts, close my eyes and tilt my head. The summer sun warms body and soul. I do not take life lightly, do I? When I was in my early twenties, similar thoughts often crossed my mind. I was not sure about motherhood. Even now, I am still not sure about how I feel. I cross the road.

I look through the glass door. There she is. Lying on her belly, head held high looking at a child sitting opposite her. Squeezing a cloth book in her tiny Buddha hands. I open the door and am greeted by the wheels of the bus. As I approach her, I call out her name, though she does not respond. I wonder when she will start recognising my voice and her name. Focussed, maybe she just did not hear me. When she sees me, I smile and a broad toothless grin lights up her face. I pick her up and give her a bear hug, "Did you have fun, my little girl?"

"She has not slept at all. We put her in bed, but no," Miriam tells me as I wrap Iqsha in the sling, as close to me as possible. A half-hearted smile, I know what this means for the rest of the afternoon. Time to head home and gear up for another long evening. I step outside, Dutch springs are pleasant, I murmur. I do not need to look down, I know. I feel the warmth of her body next to mine, her head resting peacefully on my chest. As I walk home, I know she will be with me like this till the next feed. She is sleeping so gently; how gorgeous and serene she is. Looking at her, I wonder. Will she have long curly black hair? A fair complexion and chameleon green-blue-brown eyes like her father? How many Casanovas will we have to fend off for her? Did my Amma fend off any for me? My mind wanders.

At home, I decide I might as well enjoy the outdoor warmth instead of being stuck indoors while Iqsha sleeps. I bring down memories from the attic and head out on the porch in the backyard. I lower myself onto a bench and gently rearrange her feet so as not to squash them. I lean back, her head on my chest. Such intimacy, such warmth I feel, I relish the moment. An epiphany. It has not always been this easy. I stroke the blue envelopes from Ammumma and Muthachan. Muthachan and Ammumma sent me and Chettan separate letters. Now, being a parent, I appreciate we all have our own unique relationship with others, with our children. Even though Muthachan and Ammumma were married, they did succeed in remaining two separate individuals and wrote to us siblings separately.

   I pick up a letter from Muthachan.

Dear Kamala,

Have you started reading my book?

Fifteen years later, I still have not read it and I do not think I will anytime soon. Time is such a precious commodity, especially now. Looking at Muthachan's letter, I recall the passion with which he narrated his stories. I should read his book, although I suppose I already know most stories. His trip to far off England, his travels to Malaysia and his joining the fight for freedom from the British. His scribbling brings back memories of decades ago. His stories on the veranda, me watering the plants in the evening sun, the compulsory midday nap.

I go indoors and turn on soothing Irish folk music by Clannad. I gently remove Iqsha from the sling and lay her in the cot in the living room, as softly as possible. I do not want to wake her. I know she will wake soon, I will have to change her nappy. Clannad is more for me than for her.

I hear the sound of the front door unlocking. My salvation, John is home!

"Hi love, how has she been?" John's head pokes around the corner.

I smile and hand him our bundle of Joy. Nappy time.

When John and Iqsha come downstairs, Clannad is still playing. John holds Iqsha in his arms, close to his chest. I hug them both and we waltz around the room together. I look down. ==She seems to enjoy music, since a toothless excitement lights up her face==. Lightness in our existence, lightness in our togetherness.

After dinner as I hear the sound of metal on metal I move upstairs. John, oblivious, busy with the dishes in the kitchen. I sit at my desk and pick up a pen. I open my peacock coloured scrapbook and jot down.

10th June 2020

Dearest Iqsha,

A message to my baby girl, but what to write?

10th June 2020

Dearest Iqsha,

I had never expected to become a mother. Before you were born my world was filled with adventure and bonding with people I had never met before. Now you are in my life.

You too I had never met before, but we have already started bonding. Now, when I look at you, I am grateful we have you in the heart(h) of our home. I love you to bits, and I dearly want to share my experiences and life's lessons with you.

But how?

Maybe someday I will write a book for you 😊, but for now I will try put my thoughts on paper in this letter.

I realise that this letter will contain both tears and laughter. Dear Iqsha, these life secrets are the ingredients of life I don't want to keep hidden from you. Life can get tough, reach out to the silver lining, it's always within reach. Trust in yourself and trust in others. Trust the stranger who seems helpful, he probably genuinely is!

Choose your own path and choose it wholeheartedly, and marvel at the world with all its colours! I wish you the joys of being a cultural chameleon too.

You will live and cherish your own life and the dear ones in it. You too will create your own attic of memories and your own community of belonging. Someday, I would love to open a few boxes and walk down memory lane with you. I can't wait!

Our first journey together awaits us soon. The tickets are booked. Together we will sway to the beats of salsa and gypsy music. For me it will be a trip down memory lane, for you a new world to discover and for papa it will be to enjoy with us.

My little one, I no longer can imagine my world without you.
Always yours,
Mama

Glossary

- Aguas Calientes : thermal baths (literal translation), known as Machu Picchu pueblo (village); gateway to world famous Incan ruins Machu Picchu
- Ambitabh : Amitabh Bachhan, famous Bollywood megastar
- B1G1 : buy one get one
- Bhel puris : savoury snack made of puffed rice, onions, tomatoes and tamarind sauce
- Buland Darwaza : "Door of Victory", built by Mughal emperor Akbar, the main entrance to the Jama Masjid at Fatehpur Sikri
- Caravanserais : roadside inn where travelers on the Silk Road could rest
- Chai : tea with milk, sometimes with spices such as cardamom
- Code-switching : alternating between two or more languages in a single sentence or conversation
- Cow & Chicken : American animated comedy TV series about the surreal adventures of a cow and a chicken
- Dosas : South Indian crispy pancake dish made from fermented rice and lentil batter
- Dunglish : a mixture of Dutch and English
- Dupatta : long scarf worn with a salwaar kameez
- Fatehpur Sikri : 35 km from Agra and capital city of Mughal empire under Akbar's reign
- Ghee : clarified butter
- Indira Gandhi : first woman prime minister of India
- Jamon Curado : cured ham
- Kameez : long shirt-like dress traditional Indian an Uzbeki attire
- Kathak : Indian classical dance, whose origin goes back to the band of ancient travellers of northern India known as Kathakars or storytellers
  (source Wikipedia)
- Karela : bitter gourd
- Kiwis : internationally used nickname for people from New-Zealand. The name comes from the little flightless bird that is unique to New Zealand
- Kurta pyjamas : similar to Salwar kameez
- Lassi : yoghurt drink

- Lungi : traditional Indian casual wrap-around attire for men, often white
- MacGyvering : to make or repair something in an improvised or inventive way, making use of whatever items are at hand [originated from MacGyver 1985 television series]
- Malai : milk skin formed on warm milk
- Marie Kondo : a Japanese organizing consultant, her books have sold millions of copies
- Massif Central : highland region in middle of southern France, consisting of mountains and plateaus
- MIT : Massachusetts Institute of Technology, Cambridge, USA
- Moksha : liberation from the cycle of death and rebirth, concept in many Indian religions
- Murruku : twisted deep fried savoury snack made from rice flour and lentil flour
- Nirvana : state of mind where all pain, hatred, greed, desire dissolves, enlightenment, a concept in Buddhism
- Non : flatbread
- Pachamama: goddess revered by the indigenous people of the Andes (Incas), known as the mother earth
- Pavadai : traditional dress worn mainly in South India, by girls between puberty and marriage. It consists of a long ankle-length skirt
- Pollo saltado : chicken stew
- Propeduese : Dutch university diploma issued after completion of the first year
- Pampa : Andean prairie, grassy plain
- Red Devils : name given to the Belgian football team
- Salwar kameez : traditional combination worn by Indian women; consists of a loose fitted trouser (salwar) pleated at the waist and a straight cut, below knee-length shirt (kameez)
- Samosas : deep fried pastry filled with mashed potato, onions, green peas, lentils, spices and green chili
- Sambar : South Indian lentil-based vegetable stew with tamarind
- Sangria : Spanish alcoholic drink made with red wine, chopped fruits and juice

- ✓ Sari : six yards of cloth (cotton, silk. nylon) draped over the body forming a pleated skirt and a shoulder cover up, a traditional Indian woman's attire
- ✓ Settlers of Catan : a multiplayer board game from the 1990s. Players attempt to build houses, roads and cities while acquiring and trading resources with each other
- ✓ Sol : Peruvian currency
- ✓ Somonis : Uzbeki currency
- ✓ Turbaza : holiday accommodation, Soviet era tourist camp, common in post-Soviet countries
- ✓ Vadeeee (vada), idli : South Indian snack/breakfast, a lentil doughnut fritter and a type of savoury rice cake
- ✓ Quechua : native South American language spoken in the Andes, dates back to the Incan empire in the 13th century

Translations

Amma – mother
Ammumma – maternal grandmother
Antaakshari - singing game played in India
Bomma - paternal grandmother
Buud Bazaar - Wednesday market
Chalo - come
Chappals - slippers
Chettan - brother
Coll - mountain pass
Coolies - porters at train stations
Da - yes
Darpok - coward
Didi - elder sister
Español - spanish
Gracias - thank you
Gringo or gringa - American
Haan - yes
Hola - hello
Jama Masjid - Friday mosque
Maalish - massage
Mañana - tomorrow
Muthachan – paternal grandfather
Latina - Latin American woman
Loco - crazy
Madrassa : Islamic school
Maasi - mother's sister
Mon Dieu - Oh my God
Njet - no
Pa – father
Payals - traditional anklets with bells

Pensionados - pensioners
Si - yes
Simpatico - pleasant male
Seguro - sure
señora - lady
Taqiyahs - prayer caps
Touristas - tourists
Vamos - come
Wala - fellow, man, guy
Zdravstvuyte – Hello